Best Wishes!
Mary Tatar

SEABLISS

By Mary Tatarian

PublishAmerica
Baltimore

ISBN: 978-1-4489-2760-9
PUBLISHED BY PUBLISHAMERICA, LLLP
www.publishamerica.com
Baltimore

Printed in the United States of America

Seabliss is dedicated to my husband Jerry for all of his encouragement and love.

—Mary Tatarian

CHAPTER ONE

August 10, 1986

Judy Evans fidgets in her seat waiting for Moonbeam to come out of her trance. "Ooooh," Moonbeam moans. Her head tilts from side to side as she slowly opens her eyes.

The large champagne colored candle in the center of the round table flickers so intensely one could swear that it had an on off switch.

Judy jumps at the sudden flicker. Moonbeam closes her eyes again as she feels a deep chill rushing up her spine; not exactly a good sign for a psychic. Her body jerks back as if someone is grabbing her hair from behind. Mrs. Evans watches nervously but inevitably her impatience takes over. "Moonie, what does all of this mean? Tell me, am I gonna die?"

Moonbeam is still silent. Something is passing through her body, a feeling she can't control. Moonbeam starts to speak very slowly, "Why do I feel your presence here with me? ...What's wrong?..." Her body writhes around on the chair. Her words become muffled. "Mmmm? Why should I go find her?...You're not making any sense."

The chill leaves her body as suddenly as it came and the candle extinguishes itself. Moonbeam opens her eyes to see Mrs. Evans' mouth open so wide that her jaw practically hits the table.

The psychic takes a few moments to regain her composure. "Please, Mrs. Evans, don't be alarmed. What just happened has nothing to do with you. I tried to go into a trance to see what might be in your future this coming week. Trust me, as I slipped away, I saw only beautiful flowers and boxes of sweets for you."

"Why, of course darlin', that makes perfect sense cause it's my anniversary, but you wouldn't have known that. What about all that other stuff? The moans, the words, sounds like you were havin' a pretty darn hard time. So I ain't gonna die?"

"Mrs. Evans, I guess what I'm trying to say is that your anniversary will be extra special. Please enjoy it. The rest has nothing to do with you. Now if you'll excuse me, I must make a phone call. Gray Eagle will accept your payment and schedule your next appointment. Remember, Feel the wind!"

Gray Eagle, Moonbeam's mentor and helper, escorts Judy Evans to the front room where the real business of the day is done. Moonbeam, by now frantic with worry, exits quickly to call her best friend, Mariah, who also owns a small business on the same island.

"Darn it, her line is busy. Get off that phone! I need to talk to you!"

Gray Eagle hears the ruckus as he enters the reading room, "Mrs. Beecon is here for her scheduled appointment."

Moonbeam realizes that she will have to wait until after this appointment to try her call again but doesn't like putting it off.

Moonbeam's best friend is not having a good day either. Mariah Linley steps out of her tiny office onto the floor of her video store to find her only full time employee, Shane, watching an R rated movie on the store's TV. The phone is off the hook next to his hand. Behind him and obviously unnoticed by him are four local boys aged 10 to 12 leaning over the counter to get a better look! "That's it they're all toast!" Mariah is furious as she marches over to the counter.

Staring at the boys, she means business. "OK guys, beat it, go do your homework. The show's over! Shane, take that movie out of the VCR right now! How many times do I have to tell you we play family films only in the store… In case you forgot, that's G and PG. I feel like a broken record. Don't you ever make me tell you this again."

It doesn't take a psychic to feel how stressed Mariah is as she nervously runs her fingers through her long chestnut brown hair pulling it tight at the ends.

She stands as tall as her five feet six will allow her to be. She speaks feeling herself grinding her teeth. "How hard is it? What do I have to do…tattoo the rules to your forehead?"

Mariah pauses for a few seconds, closes her large hazel eyes and takes a long deep breath. She is constantly being reminded how deep breathing calms the nerves. She starts to speak again trying her best not to yell.

"This is supposed to be a normal Friday whatever that means. I guess I'm wrong. Today, August 10th must be special because it means Shane can totally forget about rules!" Mariah cannot calm down as she fiddles through the movie receipts.

"Shane, I thought you said you checked the late slips. Look at this! Capt. Jocko is two days late with his movie. Did you call him?"

Shane, twenty-two, is a master of not letting the day-to-day stress get to him. He wears an earring in his right ear, sports a "Mom" tattoo on his left arm, and wears his long platinum streaked hair tied back neatly.

Shane begins to shake his head wildly to imaginary heavy metal music as if he is directly plugged into a band's mixer. He begins to play the "drums" on the video store's main counter using two pencils as drumsticks. To an innocent observer, it might appear that Shane could not possibly hear what Mariah has just asked him, but miraculously he responds,

"Sure have, Mariah, noooo answer."

"And you don't think it's strange for Jocko to be two days late? He's always so punctual."

Shane stops drumming and looks straight at her, "Nope, maybe he had to go back to Mexico and just forgot. Even the most conscientious make occasional mistakes. Look at me!"

Mariah's not impressed. She looks at the rental slip again. "The due date was the eighth. I'd better call him. He hates late charges…rewind fees even more since his rewinder broke. I keep rewinding his tapes for free. No point in upsetting him, you know how much he loves Spike."

Spike is Mariah's very pampered dog and official store greeter. He is currently lying near the front door of Seabliss Video, a cozy but busy little store that overlooks a beautiful stretch of Florida Gulf Coast beach, waiting for his next customer. To Mariah, anyone who loves Spike is all right in her book.

Shane rifles through the file box of phone numbers and pulls out Jocko's. He playfully hands it to Mariah even though she knows the number by heart. She quickly goes to the store phone and dials Jocko's. She has called it enough times to know that his answering machine will pick up after five rings. She holds her breath hoping she'll hear Jocko's voice.

"I hate leaving messages," She thinks as she hears the answering machine start its recorded message,

"Ahoy mates, this is your captain speaking, I'm indisposed at the moment so please leave your name and landline at the tone and I will call as soon as my old feet hit dry land."

Mariah wouldn't want Jocko to be upset with her. He's a customer but he's also a kindly old man whom she considers a friend first. Mariah remembers the first day she adopted Spike. The puppy wandered out the front door of the store unnoticed. Jocko was there and saw Mariah in tears worried about little Spike's safety. The Captain spent the next three hours combing the island only to find the little guy playing in some jasmine bushes a few blocks away. Jocko always looked out for Mariah with a fatherly eye. She knows that and now worries about him because he is older and he lives alone.

Mariah starts to leave her message; before she could get her name out, the message machine makes a strange noise as if it has reached an overload. She puts the receiver down, looking at Shane with concern. "This is very odd, not like Jocko at all. He rarely leaves town without saying good-bye to Spike and me. Must've been something pretty big."

She twists a small strand of hair as she often does when stressed and reaches for her car keys. Spike sits up at attention. He knows that he's going for a ride. "Come on boy. We're going to Jocko's. O.K. Shane, I'm sure you'll be fine. We'll be back in five or ten."

Shane dreads the words "five or ten." He knows Mariah's concept of time is equal only to her concept of accounting; both of which could qualify as a new branch of science. Shane knows that there's no point in complaining as she has a sweet way of reminding him that she signs his paycheck.

Mariah looks at her pet as she opens the glass door, "Come on Spike, let's hit the road." Spike runs out of the small island video store and jumps into Mariah's vintage 1965 red Mustang convertible. A German shepherd crossed with a teddy bear, Spike sits tall in the front seat wearing his signature red bandana and waiting for Mariah to start the engine. He loves to feel the gentile island breezes wafting through his fur.

Turning down the next corner, the easily recognizable pair head toward the Bayside Apartments. Spike begins to bark. He knows exactly where he is going and is very excited because he loves Capt. Jocko. Mariah finds a parking space in the lot that overlooks the water and the two begin to walk toward Building 1. Once there, they climb the double set of stairs that lead to Jocko's small condo.

"Hey you wait for me!" Mariah yells but Spike reaches the familiar weathered gray front door first as he always does. He sniffs the threshold and keeps sniffing obsessed with something going on behind that door.

Mariah knocks but there is no answer so she leans against the door. She can hear a faint static noise that may be coming from the TV. Spike scratches the threshold and barks at the door. "What's the matter Spike? What's wrong boy?" Determined to get in, she knocks on the door again. "Anybody home? Jocko are you there? Can you hear me?"

Still no response, so she knocks even harder, so hard that her knuckles hurt. She leans in once more pressing her ear against the door trying to distinguish the sounds, trying to hear something or someone, again only hearing very faint static.

By now, Mariah becomes incredibly concerned, "Wow, he must have had to leave quickly? Why else would he leave the TV on?" She starts to twist her hair again and talks to Spike trying to get the dog to stop barking.

"Spike, What do you hear? Oh you have no idea how I wish you could talk right now!"

Spike's continuous barking finally reaches the ears of the apartment's lazy and grouchy manager, Skip Taggert. "Will you shut that damn mutt up now?" Taggert yells as he slowly stomps up the stairs.

"I told that Jocko no more dog-sitting especially for that large unruly beast."

Taggert himself is a crusty old fisherman. Tall, with a muscular torso and shoulders, his hair is thin on top but pure white, a clear contrast to his dark beady brown eyes and leather-tanned skin. Yelling at Mariah, he limps from the top of the stairs to the doorway. Mariah always believed that his limp stemmed from a tussle with a shark. The poor shark was probably no match for the ornery Taggert.

"I can't make him stop barking." Mariah's voice pleads. "I'm sure that he's worried about Jocko. We can't get the Captain to answer the door. I'm afraid that he had to leave quickly and may have left the stove on. Maybe Spike smells smoke." Mariah hopes that the mere thought of a fire will get a reaction from Taggert. "Please, go get your passkey and let us in!"

Taggert stops dead in his tracks. "Are you crazy girl? My key is for emergencies only. I could lose my job which I'm sure that you and that excuse for a dog would love to see." Spike lifts his head, faces Taggert and growls.

"Trust me," Mariah pleads, "This is a real emergency. I can feel it. Suppose the building caught fire from the toaster or an overheated T.V.?" By now, she's grasping at straws. Taggert knocks on the door. "Jocko, stop playing hide and seek and open up this damn door!"

When Taggert gets no answer, he reluctantly pulls out his passkey. He can see signs of extreme stress in Mariah's eyes, but that doesn't bother him near as much as being accused of negligence.

He carefully places the key in the lock and slowly turns the brass doorknob. "Can this guy move any slower," Mariah thinks impatient to get inside. Finally, the door opens.

As they enter, they can hear the TV. Jocko must have left it on. Now only emitting a faint static, Mariah recognizes it as the kind of static that follows the end of a videotaped movie just before it rewinds. Despite all of the irritating electronic noise, the room seems ominously quiet and serene.

Finally inside, they see Jocko. He is sitting in a large overstuffed emerald green armchair facing the T.V.; his head is slumped forward with both of his arms out-stretched covering the wide side arms of the chair.

Spike runs to the chair and nudges Jocko's arm. The Captain does not move. Spike starts to whimper. Mariah and Taggert follow. Mariah gently shakes Jocko.

"Jocko can you hear me? Please wake up!!!"

The old Captain remains silent and very still. Mariah starts to cry. "Taggert, Hurry, Please hurry... We need to do something. Do you know CPR? Call the paramedics, He needs help and I don't know how to help him! He's so still." Mariah touches Jocko's wrist." Hurry, I can't tell whether or not he has a pulse!"

CHAPTER TWO

"Ringggggg."

"Seabliss Video, Shane speaking."

"Shane, Moonbeam. I need to talk to Mariah right now." The psychic sounds frantic.

"Good luck. She and Spike left here a little over twenty minutes ago. Who knows when I'll see her again, but I'd be happy to take a message."

"Where did they go?"

"You should know you're the psychic. Just kidding, they went to Jocko's to try and find a tape."

Moonbeam is silent. "I'll call her there." She hangs up quickly without saying another word.

Her attempt to reach Mariah, however, gets foiled again. Jocko's line is busy. She hangs up and dials the number anxiously once more as the elderly Mrs. Beecon slowly reaches the door to the reading room ready to leave. Moonbeam could not wait for the older woman to be out of the room completely before calling. Her call is by now urgent.

She can finally hear Jocko's phone ring. Her deep sigh of relief is short-lived. She is interrupted by a stranger's voice before she can complete her call.

"Step aside old woman. I need the gift of this psychic." A slim woman dressed in black pushes Mrs. Beecon out of her way to get to Moonbeam. Gray Eagle tries to keep the mystery woman outside in the foyer but there is only so much he can do.

"You have the gift, no?" The woman speaks with an accent, her face covered by layers of thin black veil. She wears a beautiful black hat.

"Do you have an appointment?" Moonbeam still has the phone in her hand even though she has hung up. She wants the woman to go away.

"No, but I am sure that you will help me. We have something or someone in common. Besides you can name your price. I need your help and guidance."

Moonbeam watches as the woman boldly walks over to the round table and sits down next to her. She touches the psychic's hand. Moonbeam tries to look into the woman's eyes through her veil, but can't. The candle in the center of the table unexpectedly extinguishes itself. Moonbeam feels a cold wind pass through the room.

"Did you feel that?" she asks.

"Feel what?" the woman responds.

"The spirit of someone you were close to in life." Moonbeam feels the wind pass through her again. She believes it to be a sign.

"Oh how wonderful! He must be here with us. I need to communicate with him. I need to feel his love."

"OK, I'll answer your questions but emergency visits are one hundred and fifty dollars." Moonbeam hopes the steep price might make the woman leave so she can call Mariah. Instead the woman opens her purse and to the psychic's surprise, takes out the necessary cash. The mysterious woman pushes the money over to Moonbeam who no longer can refuse. "OK then, let's begin." Moonbeam says closing her eyes.

Jocko's line is busy the first time Moonbeam called because the grumpy old Taggert is calling 911. His call not only reaches the volunteer emergency workers but also, in a caring town like Seabliss, magically alerts everyone else in town about what is happening at the Bayside Apartments.

"911 Operator. How may I help you?"

"Dottie, we've got an elderly man at Bayside Apartment Number Twelve. He's not breathing. Please send help now!"

A kind voice responds: "Help is dispatched. Skip is that you?"

"Yes'm. We have a problem with Captain Jocko. He's not breathing. Mariah's very upset. He needs help ASAP! We'll stay with him until they arrive."

"Skip, they're on the way."

As soon as Skip puts the receiver down, he can hear the sirens coming down Seabliss Boulevard, the main street of the island. He looks over at the motionless Captain and sees that Spike is still lying at Jocko's feet whimpering; his head is in his paws.

Mariah hears the sirens as well. In an odd way, their irritating sounds comfort her knowing that help is on the way for her good friend. Mariah wipes away her tears.

She turns from staring out the window to staring at the motionless captain. Her mind drifts back to the first day they met. He wandered into the store hoping to find a Mexican newspaper. She had no newspaper for him but tried to help him locate one. Jocko liked Mariah's attitude and became a daily visitor bringing her coffee in exchange for conversation. They soon became friends. She sighs thinking about how fast four years have past since she met the retired sea captain.

"He's so different from my other customers," she reminisces. "So dapper, so worldly, his gray hair always neatly combed back. He loves to wear his navy blazer with an emerald green silk handkerchief and walks with an incredible cane that has a silver handle in a dolphin design. I'd never met a real sea captain before and was taken in by all of his charm."

The sirens stop. Mariah is relieved as she hears the footsteps of the emergency workers on the stairs.

Bill Cranston, the deputy chief, enters the apartment first. It's his job to accompany the ambulance for safety reasons. Bill knows Mariah well sensing that she is probably in emotional distress.

"OK. We're here. We'll take over now. You just take it easy, Mariah, Let's start at the beginning Tell me what happened." He gently eases Mariah away from Jocko's chair as the paramedics immediately start to work on him.

Mariah talks to Bill who distracts her view of the proceedings. Bill knows that when Mariah is upset her information becomes unbelievably jumbled and hard to follow.

"Oh Bill, "Mariah sadly blurts out without a breath, "I was so worried about him. He's never late with his movies. I thought he went to Mexico. I don't understand why Shane didn't tell me. Anyway, I called and when I got no answer, Spike and I came over to make sure Jocko wouldn't have late charges. When Taggert opened the door, this is exactly how we found him." Tears continue to stream down her face.

Bill gently puts his arm around Mariah and gives her a brotherly hug hoping to calm her down. He then looks around the room to see Jocko on the chair surrounded by the paramedics. Spike is still whimpering at Jocko's feet. The paramedics are unsuccessful at moving the loyal dog. Jocko's trademark cane is resting against his knee.

"Bill, he's dead," one of the paramedics confirms, "I'm sorry. Looks like the old guy had a heart attack."

Bill has to be all business, "I'm sorry Mariah. We'll have to bring him back to the county morgue. Does anyone know if the Captain had any next of kin? We should notify them immediately."

Mariah wipes away her tears. "I'm pretty sure he doesn't. Spike and I were like his family here. I honestly don't know if there are any in Mexico."

Bill gently looks into Mariah's eyes, "Well, we'll have to check, honey. Poor old guy," Bill remarks as he keeps one eye on the paramedics, "Jocko may have had health problems we all didn't know about."

Mariah's hazel eyes quickly turn from tearful to focused. She is sad but becomes angry at Bill's suggestion. "Health problems? Heart attack? He looked absolutely fine and energetic the last time I saw him. He and Spike even went for a brisk walk on the beach. Jocko could outrun me! I don't understand how something like this could happen to him so quickly. Something isn't right here."

"Mariah," Bill shakes his head, "Honey, I think that you may be watching too many of your own movies. Unfortunately, things like this happen all the time. The symptoms sometimes go undetected even for strong athletes…OK boys, you can move him now."

The paramedics begin rolling the stretcher through the front door. They stop near the body and begin to open the holding straps.

"Just you wait one minute! " Mariah commands as she runs over to the chair.

"Don't you dare touch him!"

The paramedics are stunned. By her actions, one would think Mariah might be acting out of a state of shock. The paramedics know better; they've been late with tapes. She means business. They stop what they're doing simultaneously hoping for a signal from Bill.

Mariah's ability to speak with a certain air of authority makes them listen to her. Maybe that's why island folks were so surprised when she gave up her high-powered marketing job in Atlanta to come back to Seabliss and open the island's first video store.

"Don't move him, I repeat; do not. Don't contaminate the crime scene." She continues waving her arms in the air, "Do not touch a thing."

Bill walks towards her holding his head in total frustration.

"The scene of what crime?" he asks, "Mariah, you have a vivid imagination. Let him go in peace. Jocko had a heart attack. End of story."

"Sure, Bill? Bet your badge on it? I wouldn't bet the farm. I see things that don't add up."

As the two argue, Jocko's phone rings. Bill gives Mariah a look, "Don't even think about picking that up." He can see the temptation in Mariah's eyes and is relieved when it stops.

"Bill, what about his half eaten sandwich? And then there's all of the dried vomit down the front of his shirt. It actually looks like someone tried to clean it up, but I'm sure you have already taken all of that into account."

Mariah takes a deep breath as she forces herself to walk around the front of the chair again looking directly at Jocko. "'I'm doing this for Jocko, she thinks, "Look at his hands. They are facing upward and his body seems strained as if he was trying to fight off contortions...and furthermore, my deputy chief, there is no attending physician present, so my guess is that you have to treat this as suspicious until you find out otherwise...correct?"

Bill bites his tongue wishing that Mariah would go back to her real job and leave police work to him. Taggert is still standing in the apartment with his mouth open in total awe.

"You damn people make me wanna laugh." Taggert has a knack for giving his unsolicited opinion.

"We live on an island where if a sea turtle bites the dust, the whole frickin island is up in arms. Are you two that bored that you have to make up a murder? Get a life! I work on plumbing all day and I'm not as screwed up as you two. I left a clogged drain on one to let you in."

Taggert then waves his middle finger at them in disgust. Bill ignores him or he might be forced to arrest him.

CHAPTER THREE

"The last thing we all need is any more emotional outbursts. Let's all keep it cool."

"OK Mariah, let's look at your crime scene." Bill pulls his shoulders back; after all he is the one in charge. "Now don't go shootin' the messenger. Just bear with me. You're right. There's no attending physician present."

Bill does not want to be accused of being lax. A few more minutes at Jocko's will certainly not clog up his day. It's not like the deputy chief's phone is ringing off the hook.

The paramedics are still frozen in position waiting for a command from Bill to continue; but he decides to walk away from them slowly and head over to the patio doors on the other side of the room. The drapes are moving ever so slightly in the tropical breeze. With great dramatic flair, Bill pulls the silver brocade drapes open so that Mariah as well as anyone else in the room can witness the results. No one is hiding in them.

To his surprise, however, he does discover that the large sliding glass doors to the small lanai are open and the lock broken. Bill then looks down at his feet to see dirt on the threshold; the caked muddy dirt is scattered all over the lanai floor.

"Well, Mariah, I have to admit, that this is more than a bit strange." Bill sounds puzzled." Why would Jocko have the back door open, not fix a broken lock, and leave the air on? You and I both know that he was a bit of a penny pincher and what's with the dirt?"

Bill then kneels down in the doorway and picks up some of the dried mud to get a closer look.

"Wow, look at all this. It's strewn all the way to the balcony wall."

He gets up and glances back to find the red-eyed Mariah standing behind him with both arms crossed. He pauses for a few seconds as if mulling over a very tedious decision and then instructs the paramedics, "Don't touch or move anything 'til I can look around some more. There are pieces to this puzzle that just don't fit. I need to have them make sense before I leave."

The paramedics walk away from the stretcher to check their calls. They figure that they may have a bit of a wait and since the emergency has passed, they may be needed elsewhere. They know how methodical Bill is; his decisions could take minutes or hours.

Bill Cranston has been deputy police chief of Seabliss for what seems like an eternity. He always knew that he wanted a career in law enforcement and as a boy, dreamed of training to be an FBI agent. His dreams had to be set aside for reality. Bill was forced to drop out of the University of Florida for financial reasons. His grades were never good enough get a scholarship and he did not stay in school long enough to get a grasp of the forensics or justice courses needed for FBI training. He returned home to Seabliss and joined the police department.

The department consists of three officers and the chief. In a small town like Seabliss, being chief is the equivalent to being king, Bill's future promotion to the top job has many similarities to Prince Charles' promotion; both have to wait for someone to die. On a more positive note, Bill's job rut does not affect his job performance. He is a sharp guy.

Nor does it stop the local ladies' interest in him. Bill is still single, in his late thirties, about the same age as Mariah, and possesses an undeniable boyish charm. They dated in high school but parted ways when college beckoned. Local gossip still sees a spark between them. Bill's sandy blond hair shows slight signs of gray contrasting a well-tanned complexion derived from patrolling the beach. Tall, he looks ever so good in his khaki short-sleeved uniform shirt with navy Bermuda length shorts.

Bill continues, "Damn shame this had to happen to Jocko. Hell of a nice guy!"

He's talking to himself in an effort to both keep Mariah calm and limit her questions. Technically, she's not even supposed to be there. He understands that she was the one to find Jocko. "If I try to kick her out, she'll make a scene. Gotta keep the lid on things." Bill utters to himself as he walks slowly around Jocko's chair one more time. If no one else complains, he'll let Mariah stay to help her absorb what has just happened. He stops short as if finding something important.

Mariah watches as he pulls a small pair of needle nose pliers from his back pocket.

"Well, lookee here kids."

He removes a small cigarette butt hiding behind the left leg of Jocko's trousers.

"Guess the old guy had company; we just don't know who." Bill holds up his find for everyone to see. "If I'm not mistaken, Jocko only smoked a pipe!" Bill looks at one of the paramedics, also as a police officer.

"Hey Brady go down to my car and bring up my toolbox. Then get on the radio and call headquarters. Ask Johnson to come back here with his camera and while you're at it, call Doc. Tell him that we'll need the M.E. He'll make the call for us. Can't be too sure about anything now" Bill tosses Brady his car keys.

Mariah breathes a deep sigh of relief. Bill seems to believe her. She wipes away her tears.

"Sooo, Bill maybe I'm right" Mariah asks gently.

Bill is proceeding cautiously. "Nope, Didn't say that Mariah, Just making sure we don't overlook anything. Chief Donner sure hates law suits."

Brady comes back inside and hands the toolbox over to Bill who opens the rusty red metal case and takes out some rubber gloves. He puts them on and picks up the cigarette butt with his needle nose pliers and places it in a clear plastic bag. As he runs his hands on the floor near where the cigarette was found, he can hear a car door slam followed by footsteps. Officer Johnson has just arrived with the camera.

"Hey Johnny boy, not too much going on the rest of the island, huh? We need you to use your photo skills and shoot this scene."

Johnson walks around the room flash charging and firing as fast as he can shoot. He photographs Jocko, the floor, the patio doors, and the bedroom. The bright lights are enough to make everyone in attendance see spots. Johnson finishes and then leaves. After all, someone has to be on call. Bill sends Brady back down to the squad car to get the yellow crime scene tape. Once in his hands, Bill starts to surround the small condo with the bright yellow tape as if putting a garland on a Christmas tree. Just then, Bill and Mariah hear another car door slam. Brady lifts his head over the yellow tape and says,

"Must be the M.E. That was super quick. He must have been on the island already for him to get here this fast."

The medical examiner works for the county. In the height of tourist season it could take over an hour for him to drive from town to the island; but his entrance is speedy even for August.

The tape separates and a man walks through the garland. Mariah looks up surprised to see that it's Doc Tranor, Seabliss' only physician.

"Hey Bill, the M.E. is cruising the fiords of Norway, the assistant M.E. is in Acapulco at an international medical convention, so I guess that makes me acting medical examiner. Great huh? Whatcha got?"

Obviously, by the sound of his voice, Doc is not enthused. Bill and Mariah are totally surprised. "I was," Doc continues," kind of hoping nothing would happen on my watch. I have three days left until the assistant M.E. comes home and got roped into this assignment as a favor to him."

Bill smiles at that thought but regains his composure so that he can explain what he thinks may have happened to Jocko.

"Well Doc, this may be nothing…Jocko may have just had a heart attack but Mariah suspects foul play and I've found some suspicious bits in the room…"

Doc pulls up the collar of his trademark Hawaiian shirt and asks, "And when did the chief give Mariah a homicide badge? No offense, Mariah, but as everybody else in town tells you, it's not good for you to watch so many movies."

Mariah is getting a little sick of people criticizing her job." Why do people think all I do is watch movies? Try it for a day, Doc, it's not as easy as you think." She then looks at Doc and in a matter of fact way repeats her talking points:

"Listen to me, you know more than anyone else on this island that Jocko was in the best of health. Look around the room; look at him. His lunch is half eaten, it looks like someone tried to clean the vomit up, and what about the fact that the sliders are open and the air conditioner on. You know how frugal Jocko was. Bill found a cigarette butt near Jocko's feet. As you know, Jocko smoked a pipe. And then there is the matter of the twisted position of his body. This, my good doctor, ain't no movie!" Mariah begins to twist that trademark handful of curls as she speaks.

Doc's face reflects the fact that he does not like what he is hearing.

"You think this is a suspicious death because of a cigarette butt and vomit. Girl you really need to take more time off…but to placate both of you and, since Bill called me in an official capacity, I will have a look at the body."

Doc walks over to Jocko's body.

"Look at his arm, Doc!" Mariah sees something she did not see before. *Doc* was still looking at Jocko's position.

"Mariah, the position of the body and his demeanor are consistent with that of a heart attack victim. He probably had it while eating lunch after he had company. Maybe he had intended to close the door but never had the chance to make it over there."

Mariah bites her tongue.

"OK, Doc, then what about his right arm?"

"Mariah," Doc sounds almost scolding," I hope you didn't touch the body."

"Doc, his sleeve was already rolled up. Look at his arm."

Doc leans in closer to the victim's arm. "Needle marks…huh! Well we all know that Jocko was a diabetic. He gave himself insulin shots."

Mariah is peeved.

"Yes Doc, we all know that, but Jocko was never this messy. Look at his veins… they have all collapsed. The skin near the needle marks has turned yellow and purple blue. Doc, Jocko knew where to put his needle and was always neat."

"Well, Mariah" Doc answers, "Maybe he was in the midst of having a heart attack and missed."

"Let's get real. Looks like somebody tried to clean up the vomit. I just walked around the body once and saw that. And, by the way, he doesn't smell too great."

"Well, Mariah." Doc adds, "The poor old guy is dead."

"No Doc, not that, I mean like poop to use a polite term."

Spike hears the word "poop" and lifts his head.

Doc tries to reason with her. "It's not unusual to have vomiting and bowel release at the time of death. By the levidity of the body, he was not moved. Jocko died in this chair.

Rigor mortis has begun to set in because it appears that he has been dead a little over one day. Jocko's mouth is open because the muscles in his jaw have given out."

The only thing I can't explain," Doc continues, "Is why some of the vomit has been cleaned up."

Bill listening quietly adds, "Doc I'm just a meager deputy police chief but I've never heard of a dead man cleaning up his own vomit. Humor us here. This could very likely be a suspicious death. I think we should all proceed with that in mind."

"I intend to dust for prints especially near the coffee table and the glass sliders. I've already bagged the butt and had Johnson take photos. I want nothing touched. And as for you, Doc Temporary M.E, there was no attending physician at the time of death so I want a full post mortem examination."

Now Doc is definitely not a happy camper.

"I was afraid of that. Bill. I've lived in Seabliss for a long, long time. Sometimes I think too long. We have stingray bites, spider bites, sun poisoning and tourist flu. Jocko was an old man who had a sudden heart attack. Except for the vomit being cleaned up I think you both are under too much stress! Well, I suppose if you need an autopsy and toxicology reports, the assistant M.E. will be back in a few days. I'll make sure to tell him to take care of this case first."

'Doc," Bill replies, "We can't wait that long. We need this info now. If this is a murder, the quicker we have the information the quicker we might apprehend the murderer. He, she or they may still be in Seabliss."

Doc is silent. He takes a very deep breath.

"Look Bill I'm just covering as a favor for Manny Ladde, the assistant M.E. I owe him this. I'm just a country doctor who hates doing autopsies. I repeat the word hates in case you missed that the first time."

Bill is sympathetic but firm, "Didn't miss it Doc. But we owe it to Jocko and we owe it to the town to know if a murder has been committed. Who would murder such a nice old guy? This person may do it again to any of us."

Mariah looks surprised at Doc's answer.

"You hate autopsies! What kind of excuse is that? I hate to splice tapes and listen to whiney reasons why people are late but it's part of my job."

"True Mariah, but splicing does not produce vulgar odors and terrible scenes of body parts and organs."

Doc looks at Jocko's arm again.

"These needle marks do look strange. They are all discolored and the fact that the vomit is cleaned up I guess we need to do some homework. But I repeat, my professional opinion is that Jocko had a heart attack so don't go causing panic in the general population. Understand?" Bill nods as he gives instructions.

"O.K. guys, I guess we can move him now. Take him to the county morgue where Doc can take a closer look at him."

The paramedics carefully lift Jocko from the chair and gently place him in the black body bag. They then lift him onto the stretcher and start to wheel him out the door. Mariah and Spike follow the stretcher to the top of the stairs.

"Are you O.K. to drive Mariah?" Bill asks.

"I guess." Mariah replies fighting back tears. Spike stands very still at her side.

Bill gives her a hug.

" Gotta run to make sure we find out what really happened to Jocko. Be careful. I'll let you know what's going on."

Mariah shakes her head.

"Poor Jocko. As far as I know, he has no family here. What should I do? Jocko was so loved, why would anyone want to harm him"

"Mariah, Don't worry," Bill consoles her. "I'll help you figure it all out. Just go back to your store, I'll call you there."

He runs down the stairs, jumps in the patrol car. The car peels out of the small parking lot. Bill turns on his blue lights excited to indicate that he is on official police business. He may actually have a real case.

Mariah and Spike watch from the top of the stairs. She turns slowly and realizes that Taggert left the scene unnoticed. "I'm so upset I'm not paying attention to anything else. Guess I'd better start if I want to find who did this."

CHAPTER FOUR

The mysterious woman in black gets up from the table anxious to leave Moonbeam's reading room.

She looks pleased by what Moonbeam has told her. Moonie, however, remains seated. She is silent and deep in thought, unaware of the woman's departure. Grey Eagle has to come to escort her out.

He looks at Moonbeam concerned over the psychic's unusual demeanor. He notices that she is clutching an ornate sterling silver locket, one that he has never seen before and one that she keeps hidden under multiple chains of crystals.

Grey Eagle comes right back in to check on Moonbeam. "Are you OK? Hey snap out of it."

Moonbeam shakes her head as if trying to get rid of cobwebs. She does not let go of the necklace.

"This is my great great grandmother Martha's locket. The "M" on the heart means even more to me now that my chosen name is Moonbeam.

That woman wanted to touch it, to look at it more closely. I don't know how she even knew I even had it on. I keep it hidden because my grandmother told me that it had powers. Special powers for those chosen to wear it and those powers diminish if touched by a non-believer. I had to protect my powers.'

Gray Eagle just watches stunned by her revelation. This is something even he did not know about his friend.

"It's all right Moonbeam. She's gone."

Moonbeam slowly releases her hand letting the heart-shaped locket go. She had grabbed the heart with the letter "M" engraved on it by its side. As the locket fell back on its chain, she could feel the palm of her hand burning. She looks down at her hand. The "M" sideways left a deep imprint that looks like the number three.

"Three? Could my locket be trying to tell me something? Three? I must call Mariah now. Grey Eagle get me the phone please. I feel totally drained."

Grey Eagle leaves and brings her the phone. Mariah dials Jocko's number one more time.

Moonbeam isn't the only one feeling drained. Poor Doc hasn't even started yet and he would like to call it a day as he follows Bill and the ambulance to the county morgue. The police lights, although no brighter than usual, seem blinding for the easy going doctor as he follows the sad caravan in his silver Jaguar sedan. Poor Doc is deep in thought about everything that has just happened and what is now expected of him. His thoughts become so intense that they make him speak aloud.

"Everybody I know knows. I know they know. I hate to perform autopsies. Why did I ever agree to cover for that damn assistant M.E.? Well, I guess he did bale me out a few times with believable excuses for my ex. Now, he's gone and I have a mere three days left on his watch and Jocko has to die suspiciously and if that's not bad enough, I have to do the autopsy. If Jocko had to die, why couldn't he wait three days?"

Doc grips his steering wheel with both hands as he goes over the day in his mind.

"There I was sitting peacefully on my porch just watching the water and sipping a well deserved Margarita when the phone rings. I hear my answering machine pick up. It's Brady."

Doc always uses an answering machine when off duty to screen his calls. Seabliss, like any other town, has its share of hypochondriacs.

"Doc it's Deputy Brady. Bill needs you to pick up. We've got an emergency"

"I still can't believe the nerve Brady has in asking me to pick up. He knows that when my machine is off so am I. It even gives instructions 'In case of an emergency call 911 or Sand County emergency room 668-2310.' He must be deaf or dense or I was stupid to pick up. Now, I have to pay the price. I never should have answered that call! Never!"

"What am I going to do? Haven't done anything like that since med school where I almost passed out. This isn't why I became a doctor."

Doc takes a deep breath. A slow chill runs up his spine even though the thermometer reads ninety-two degrees.

Doc has been the only physician practicing on Seabliss since he moved to this sleepy island paradise some twenty years ago hoping to escape from the hustle of big city living and big city medical problems. Tranor took to island living immediately and so did his practice. He treats infections from sunburn, stingray bites, as well as colds imported from up North. Doc checks out the locals for yearly exams but sends them elsewhere if he discovers any kind of problem that he can't treat easily.

He quickly tired of the shirts and ties he wore in his former life. His new attire of choice, brightly colored Hawaiian shirts and khaki Bermuda shorts, soon became his trademark uniform.

Doc's large beachfront residence, a weathered old Southern style home, also serves as his office. The spacious and light front room serves as a waiting area comfy enough for the locals and unique enough for tourists. "I like to give them a good story to take home with my bill," Doc always brags. He converted the original dining room and den into examination rooms while the waterfront kitchen serves as a small lab. His personal residence is upstairs.

When Doc first arrived in Seabliss, he was not alone. As he tells anyone who will listen, "I came with my fashionable and expensive wife, Susan." Susan was a definite type-A personality who truly enjoyed spending hours keeping up with the Joneses. She found his new lifestyle extremely frustrating and upsetting. She would constantly ask, "How on earth can you expect me to live in no-man's land. There's not even a mall for twenty five miles!"

Doc's lack of ambition and choice of office location finally drove her over the deep end. One day, after Doc returned home from hospital visits, he found a totally empty house. She packed all of her things and most of his, had the furniture moved, and left. Soon thereafter, she filed for divorce draining whatever finances he had saved to that point. Doc would whine, "That selfish pig! She even took my dog!"

It is totally understandable why Doc is still gun-shy of any permanent relationship. With his tall lanky frame and slightly graying chestnut hair, women of all ages, tourists and locals alike, feel that he is a real catch. "I guess I'm lucky, I can have my pick." Doc tries to rationalize his uncomfortable position.

But for the present, he is perfectly happy dating a beautiful young lady named Moonbeam, the local psychic. She believes, a belief that has been reinforced by the stars, that they make quite a team. She often reminds him that, "You my darling heal the body while I heal the soul."

All of Doc's scattered thoughts cannot shut off those flashing lights as the ambulance turns the corner that leads to the back entrance of Sand General County Hospital. The Medical Examiner's building is located to the rear of the hospital parking lot.

Finally off, the pulsating red lights are no longer a distraction to Doc. He parks his Jaguar and walks over to the ambulance which waits near the entrance of the ME's building. He slowly gives the paramedics directions.

"Take Jocko in that entrance and straight ahead to the morgue to check in. I'll call for an immediate autopsy. I'll meet you there." As he points directions to the paramedics, Doc can feel a presence behind him. He turns around and sees Bill.

"Bill, I'll go on in ahead and make arrangements for the autopsy. Damn shame about Jocko. Fine fellow. He's always been one of my favorite patients. Can't lie buddy, I'm really not looking forward to this."

Bill looks at Doc almost sympathetically, "I know Doc but I have a funny feeling Mariah may be right. She actually may have hit on something when she found the bruised needle marks and cleaned up vomit. Jocko injected insulin carefully and on a daily basis. He was too proud to admit that he had a health problem. His arms were rarely discolored from missed veins. Maybe a stab in the dark, no pun intended, but I have a hunch Jocko didn't die naturally. If Jocko was murdered, I'm going to catch whoever killed him."

Doc looks serious, "I understand. I'll call as soon as the tests are complete."

"No Doc,' Bill interrupts, "I'm gonna stay and watch. I've witnessed an autopsy in my one and only forensics class. This way I'll know what you find as soon as possible. Except for the lab, of course."

Doc's mouth is wide open; he is stunned and totally speechless. He did not see this coming. He shudders at the thought of getting sick in front of Bill. Nervously, Doc pulls his shorts up and starts walking very slowly down the corridor to the morgue.

Bill follows Doc with an authoritative gait. They manage to turn a few heads along the way, Doc in his red Hawaiian shirt and shorts, Bill in his deputy's uniform and gun belt.

Bill is extremely anxious to find out what really happened to Jocko. Yesterday is not soon enough. After all, this may be the first murder Seabliss has seen in years and it happens to be on his watch. As he opens each of the large hospital sized corridor doors, he starts to sprint down the short sterile

hallway to the Medical Examiner's Offices where the County Morgue and
M.E.'s examining rooms are located.

To any casual observer, they do look like an extremely odd duo. Bill is crisp,
muscular and professional looking in his uniform, while Doc is more than a bit
frazzled, and dressed very casually.

Right now, each could care less what others think; they are on a mission.
Bill soon pushes open the two heavy doors to the compact morgue and then
opens the ones to the adjacent autopsy room.

Doc is lagging but not too far behind, "Wow, am I out of shape. I can't keep
up with him. I'm out of breath just watching him sprint from the parking lot."

Unbeknownst to Doc, much of Bill's energy stems from the fact that he too
would like to get this horrible duty over with. Bill is not thinking straight. He
opens the doors so quickly that they almost slam right into an out of breath Doc
who is still hot on his heels.

Doc stops for a minute and bends over as if to catch his breath much like
a runner after a big race. He pauses and looks up at Bill. "If there is any breath
left in my old body, I'll be able to scrub and put on a gown. Do you want to do
the same or watch through the observation window?"

"I'll watch through the window," Bill quickly replies. "Remember. Doc, all
of Jocko's clothes and possessions have to go to the county crime lab. O.K.?"

"O.K." Doc answers abruptly.

"If anyone hurt Jocko in any way, we want to catch this person. This is now
personal. The longer the time this animal has to elude us, the more likely he'll
never be caught."

"Cool it, Bill. We haven't even established that there was a crime."

Bill takes off his deputy chief baseball cap as a sign of his respect for Jocko,
"Well, that's exactly why we're all here. Now, Doc, let's get to it." Bill enters
the observation room.

Doc walks as if in slow motion to the scrub area. He comes back prepared
but obviously not very happy. He raises his white sterile gloves as a signal to
Ted. As Bill and Doc watch, Ted, the morgue's only full time attendant, wheels
the stainless steel gurney carrying Jocko's remains into the room.

CHAPTER FIVE

Mariah and Spike are still waiting quietly in Jocko's apartment. "Oh Spike it's hard to leave knowing that we'll never see Jocko here again. I'm just not ready yet," Mariah croons as she pets her dog's head.

They both watch intently as Johnson, the returning deputy to the scene, finishes collecting anything that might be seen as evidence.

As Johnson leaves, he drapes the front doorway with yellow crime scene tape. Mariah is still very upset and reverts to uncontrollable bouts of crying.

"Hey, Mariah, you O.K. to drive? Johnson asks kindly "Need a lift back to the store? I'll even let ol' Spike ride in my squad car" he chuckles in a kindly manner.

"No Thanks. I'll be all right in a few minutes. I just have to be strong about this. Spike and I both loved Jocko. He's very dear to both of us."

Mariah looks up from her layers of damp tissue to notice that Johnson cannot find the key to lock the apartment door. "Of course, Taggert is nowhere to be found when you really need him," she thinks.

Johnson fiddles with the front door, but realizing that there is little he can do to rectify that situation, goes to the back door where he left a long piece of wood that he found in another room. He screws it across the back door frame from the inside. He hopes that his efforts will keep intruders out from the back until he can return with a better resolution. He then instructs Mariah.

"O.K. Mariah, Jocko's place is as secure as I can get it for now. When you leave, you can lock the front door by turning the lock on the inside knob. I'll return with the key that Bill probably forgot he had in his pocket. You really shouldn't be here. I'll give you a few moments alone as a friend but don't under any conditions let the chief know I did this for you. And do not I repeat do not touch anything! I'll be back in a few as soon as I find Bill. Don't hesitate to call for that ride. Losing one good neighbor in a day is enough for everyone. Be careful."

"Thanks. We will." Mariah responds to his kindness.

With that Johnson scampers quickly down the stairs.

Mariah watches from the upstairs window as he gets into his vehicle. No sooner than Johnson pulls out of the parking lot then Jocko's phone rings. Mariah runs to the kitchen and opens one of the cabinets. She knows where Jocko keeps the box of rubber gloves, opens the box and puts on a pair.

She waves from the window as Johnson drives off counting to five before answering the phone.

She picks up the receiver but does not answer.

"Mariah, Moonie, are you all right?"

"No. No, I'm not. Far from it. It's Jocko. He's dead."

"Dead? Oh my… I'm so sorry, honey. That must have been his spirit who came to me during a reading. The spirit said that it was urgent. He wanted me to find you so desperately."

Mariah forgets about her grief for a few seconds, puzzled by Moonbeam's last statement.

"His spirit? Moonie cut the fluff. It's me you're talking to. You've never been visited by a spirit in your life, unless you count the island Christmas pageant where you volunteered to break the sex barrier and portray Scrooge as a medium."

"Mariah, I am dead serious. Oops no pun intended. Something came over me in the middle of one of my readings. It possessed me. My mind left my body…"

"That's not new," Mariah laughs feeling a bit guilty that she could laugh after such a tragedy.

"Let me finish. My mind left my body. I saw Jocko. He was standing in a haze of bright light."

"His hand reached out to me. I pulled back and started to come to, but he pulled me back in.

In a serious voice he said, 'There are evil people who harmed me. They are still out there. You must warn Mariah.'

"Why didn't you tell me?"

"I tried several times but ran into busy signals, no answers, and more clients. I am so very sorry. He was a good friend to both of us."

"So, then what happened?"

"His hand let go of mine. I awoke to see Mrs. Evans with her jaw open so wide she could swallow a balloon, but it didn't end there. Later a rich woman dressed in black barged her way into my reading room. I felt that spirit pass through the room again. This time I clutched my great great grandmother's locket, the one with the "M" engraved on it. The "M" stamped a three on my palm."

Moonbeam is quiet hoping that she didn't upset Mariah anymore than she already was.

"Moonie, an M sideways can be mistaken for a three."

"Mariah that's a spiritual necklace. It has powers. I may really have the gift. The three was a message from beyond."

"OK if it makes you happy but there are rational explanations for both. What did that woman want from you anyway?"

"It was very strange. She asked two esoteric questions. I answered yes to both and she left. Go figure."

"Moonie, now I'm not sure what to do. If it walks like a duck, the duck, named murder, is quacking loudly in my ear. If I accept your story, then…"

"What do you mean accept my story? Why would I try so hard to reach you?"

"I mean," Mariah continues, "You have in your own way corroborated my theory. It's like pulling teeth to get Bill and Doc on board."

"What can I do to help? Do you want me to come over? Maybe talk to Doc or Bill?"

"No, they already left with Jocko's body. I'm not supposed to stay here. Just hang in there and don't tell anyone about our conversation. It's better, at least in the beginning, if one knows that we'll be working together. I'll call you as soon as I can."

"Mariah, be careful. Remember feel the wind."

The two friends hang up. Mariah knows that she must work faster to find out anything at all before the deputy returns to lock up the apartment. She pulls out her all in one Swiss Army knife and mini tool kit from her purse.

"Never know when you have to unscrew the top of a VCR," Mariah thinks," Let's see, I need a Phillips head screwdriver. Aha."

She twists the screws and takes off the top looking over one shoulder to make sure that no one sees her.

"Well, Spike, I guess the first thing we should do is get the tape out of the VCR. In all of the confusion, that is the one thing they overlooked."

With the top off, she gently lifts the stuck tape from its holder.

"Huh, look at this. How ironic that the last movie Jocko would watch is

'Appointment With Death'. I saw the title on the slip but it didn't register 'til now."

She carefully puts the tape in her purse as her attention turns to the sliding back door.

"Spike, you and I both know that if the police get their hands on this tape I won't get it back for months. We're sad about Jocko but he most of all would want us to be prudent."

"Wow how strong can that little Johnson be?" Mariah asks as she struggles to unscrew the board. She manages to pry it off gently so as not to disturb any of the other surroundings. Mariah then lifts the side of the long board holding the door shut over her head and slips underneath it and out into the lanai.

After what Mariah just experienced, this once familiar view of the harbor filled with shrimp and fishing boats now casts an ominous shadow. She starts to twist that one side of her hair as she looks around the little screen room hoping to find a clue.

Spike starts pacing nearby and sniffs the sliders rather intently.

Mariah watches him. He is still near the sliding glass doors.

"I don't understand. Why leave a door open with the air on?" Spike is sniffing very loudly.

"Someone else was here. Huh Spike... Who was it?"

Spike starts scratching at the lanai floor near the sliders. "With all of the fingerprint dusting, how come no-one thought of checking the back slider from the outside?"

Mariah carefully picks up a second cigarette butt using the mini pliers from her tool kit that is lying on the floor next to the dog. She is careful not to touch it. "I'll go get another baggy from the box. Hmmm...Were there were two people here or only just one murderous chain smoker?"

Mariah turns and faces the water. "There are no stairs in the back. On this old building, the only escape is with a rope ladder."

"Whoever came in, "Mariah continues, "came in through the front door. Nothing in the entrance was tampered with. That means that it probably was someone Jocko knew. He or she had to have been here before and knew the lay of the land. Maybe that person opened the lanai for a smoke or to hide until Jocko came home for lunch? Or maybe that's how he or she left?"

Mariah knows she has to hurry but she just can't control her curiosity She goes back inside, replacing that board on the closed sliders ever so carefully and then starts poking around in the small kitchenette that opens to the main room of the apartment.

She quickly notices a basket on the counter with some unopened mail. Mariah does not want to touch anything so she tilts her head sideways to see that the first postmark is from Mexico. Mariah twists her hair. "Mexico" she says out loud. Her curiosity once again gets the better of her. She listens to make sure that no one is approaching the apartment and then opens her purse and digs out a pair of tweezers. She then opens one of the small kitchen cabinets where she knows that Jocko keeps the teapot. She is still wearing rubber gloves as she fills the pot with water to boil for steam. With the tweezers, Mariah carefully pulls the first letter from Mexico out from the stack of bills. Mariah knows that Jocko liked to spend three to four months a year in a small village on the Gulf coast. It appears that the letter had already been opened making Mariah's snooping so much easier.

She extracts the pale pink stationery from the envelope and starts to read; "My love," Mariah is grateful that the letter is written in English since she is not fluid in Spanish. "Everyday that we are apart is like a year. I need to write to you because our village is in trouble and I need to know what to do."

"Luis and his men are terrorizing the workers as well as myself. He said he would get you too for what you did to him. Be careful my love. Stay safe.
ANNA"

"Anna" thought Mariah, "I know Jocko had someone special in Mexico but now she has a name."

Mariah examines the outside of the envelope. There is no return address just a postmark "Ojuana, Mexico." She carefully puts the letter back in the envelope. As she returns the envelope to the basket, she notices some bills also mailed from Mexico mixed in with Jocko's local ones. Mariah stops for a minute but then picks up the bills. They too have already been opened.

"Thank goodness Jocko was so organized"

It appears that the first is a bill for electricity in a place of business. Mariah has a limited knowledge of Spanish but she can understand that it is for some kind of factory in Ojuana.

The second bill shows a physical address.

"Where the heck is Ojuana?" Mariah wonders as she folds the papers carefully and puts them back in their proper envelopes. Just as she is finishes, she hears a noise. Startled, she looks up as she hears the front door opening very slowly.

CHAPTER SIX

Mariah Annabel Linley is no shrinking violet. She rarely lets fear get the better of her, but very few things in her life so far have prepared her for this overwhelming feeling of dread.

She's weathered some tough times in the past but has always managed to land on her own two feet. Mariah is no stranger to the island; she's local and proud of it. She enjoys telling her story to any tourist who'll listen.

"I was born here thirty seven years ago. I moved away once but have no intention of ever leaving again. I went to the one room island grammar school and am a proud alum of county high. My Dad was the best. He worked hard as a shrimp boat captain. Needless to say, my Mom and I were devastated when he drowned after his boat and crew ran into a no name storm at sea. I was ten and felt totally lost without him"

"Instead of my family shrinking, it grew. All of our wonderful neighbors saw something special in me. I went to the University of Miami with the help of beach scholarships. There, I majored in advertising and, after graduating with honors, decided to try my luck in the dog eat dog business world of big city Atlanta."

"I made a lot of money but I missed my island life and of course my island family who made all that possible for me.

"I came back about six years ago. I saved enough money to buy my cottage but my biggest problem was finding a job. That was the hard part. I knew my options were slim so I decided to start my own business. So many people told me that I was crazy. Why a video store? I guess I've never been afraid to take a chance and so Seabliss Video was born."

The islanders loved her new venture and soon adopted it as their own. Even with the enormous influx of tourists, the store never lost its hometown flavor.

"I felt like buying a pot belly stove, of course not for heat, but because my store became a gathering place. Islanders love to come in and talk about impending storms, local gossip and of course any sightings of visiting celebrities."

Since Jocko lived alone, he, like so many of the other older single islanders, enjoyed visiting Mariah's store on a daily basis when he was in town. He shared stories about his latest travels to

Mariah never pried into why he visited Mexico so often. She always sensed that there was more to his story then he led others to believe.

The older ladies of the island, many of whom found the Captain quite attractive, enjoyed discussing the possibility of his having romantic trysts in Mexico as an explanation for his frequent visits. Before Jocko's death, Mariah would just listen to them and snicker. "After all," Mariah thinks, "These same ladies say similar things about Bill and me," But now having found that letter from Anna, Mariah is not so sure that the ladies' stories are that far off.

"Jocko was like a father to me. He took an interest in what I did. He always tried to give me good advice." Mariah is comforted by the thought that the Captain really cared about her.

That feeling is now her biggest motivation. She feels compelled to find out what really happened to her friend. Jocko never had a daughter. Mariah must fill those shoes and follow through as painful, unnerving and dangerous it might be for her.

Moonbeam, who knows Mariah better than anyone, has often told her, "You have such determination and inner strength. I'm sure that in one of your past lives, you were a great warrior princess. You bravely charged into battle, defeating your enemies and carrying your flag with pride." Of course, Mariah would just shrug off Moonie's comments.

Now as that door slowly squeaks open, Mariah wishes the warrior princess in her would surface.

CHAPTER SEVEN

Mariah gets up slowly. She stands silently with her back to the front door. The solid wooden door slowly scrapes open. Her heart starts to pound; her mind starts to race." Suppose it's the chief?" She gasps, "Suppose it's the killer coming back to look for something?"

Mariah, frozen stiff, is afraid to turn around. Spike moves to stand in back of her for protection. She hears the footsteps of someone entering the small condo. She knows she must be brave. This visitor will either place her in danger or in jail.

Mariah takes a deep breath, holds it as she slowly turns around to face the front door. "Grrrrrr," Spike utters sensing her fear. "I'm in for it now." Mariah worries," I hope Spike's growl doesn't mean bad things for my future. I'm afraid to look."

The door finally opens all of the way. Mariah sees the head of a short well-tanned man making his way through the crime scene tape. He peers around the condo with an intimate sense of familiarity but remains guarded as if he knows that he is not supposed to be there. Mariah turns to take a closer look.

"Whew, that's not the chief or anybody else from the police department. I probably shouldn't, but I need to move nearer the door to see if I recognize him. My curiosity will probably kill me some day but I really really hope today won't be that day."

She maneuvers herself to get a closer look at the man. He's older. Extremely limber, he has an easy time of walking under the yellow crime tape. Mariah notices that he is stocky sporting a well-groomed mustache. He shows no remorse about moving the crime tape to clear a path as he walks through Jocko's apartment. Entering the living room with confidence, Mariah suspects that he may be searching for something in particular. The man suddenly looks up. Surprised, his eyes meet Mariah's. To her astonishment, he steps back startled as if he is afraid of her. He clears his throat. "Ahem, excuse me senorita, I am looking for Senor Jocko?"

The older gentleman appears puzzled. "I walked over to visit him when I see all the lights and the police automobiles. Then I hear sirens. Is Captain Jocko all right?"

Mariah looks into his tired black eyes. Her eyes begin to swell with tears. Without her even speaking a word, the old man senses that Jocko is gone. He sits down suddenly almost falling on a stool near the kitchen counter. He places his head in his hands.

"I'm so sorry" Mariah whispers trying to console him. "Were you a close friend of Jocko's?"

The man lifts his face slowly from his hands. His eyes are red with tears. He breathes a deep sigh as he takes a sterling silver cigarette case from his inside jacket pocket. He opens it, removes a cigarette, and lights it.

"Forgive me. I should introduce myself," he begins as he inhales. My name is Pacco. I work for Senor Jocko in Mexico. Senor Jocko is very good to me and my family. He called me a week ago and said that he needed me here for a little while to help him. He said he had to go back to Mexico to fix something. So of course I come here on his boat right away."

Mariah remains silent, as she is intrigued beyond words. She listens intently thinking, "Jocko had a double life. Wait until Moonie gets a load of this."

She smiles kindly at Pacco. Her smile is genuine, very charismatic; she knows that just the flash of it makes people trust her.

"You worked for him in Mexico?" she asks hoping he'll continue, "Funny he never mentioned you to me…"

Pacco looks into Mariah's kind eyes. She senses that he is comfortable with her, "Si, senorita, I work in his factor. I have worked for him for almost two years!

"We make many beautiful things. Captain Jocko is family to me."

Mariah, eager to learn more, doesn't want to upset the old man any more than necessary.

"Do you know Anna?" she asks remembering the names from the letter.

"Si" He shakes his head up and down smiling.

"Do you know a man named Luis?"

The old man sits perfectly still and remains silent. His face and demeanor are framed with fear.

"It is better not to know Luis if you follow me, senorita."

Mariah sits up straight on the barstool. She isn't quite sure where to go next with her questioning but knows that she needs more answers to quench her thirsty curiosity.

In times of stress, Mariah's mind reverts to movies. What would the greats like Charlie Chan, Sherlock Holmes, and Hercule Poirot ask? "Their words wouldn't sound right coming from me. I better stay with what works," she thinks. She decides to use her discreet but successful technique for locating missing videos.

Mariah's soft hazel eyes gaze deeply into Pacco's. "You know, I never introduced myself. My name is Mariah."

Pacco has trouble pronouncing her name," Si Maria. Jocko tells me about you. Very nice."

She continues, "He was like a father to me. I will miss him. Jocko told me how much he loved Anna. I just wish that I could have met her. Jocko invited me to go to Mexico many times and visit with them, but I always had to work. Anna must be quite a wonderful woman. Please, tell me all about her. If you would give me her address, I would like to write a letter of sympathy to her and offer to send her Jocko's personal things if she would like."

Pacco appears deeply touched by Mariah's gesture of kindness.

"That is kind of you. My dear, there is so much to tell you about both of them. I do not know where to start."

Mariah smiles as she speaks softly. "Let's start at the beginning. I want to hear all about their love story."

Pacco puts his cigarette out in an ashtray on the counter "O.K. It's a very beautiful one. I will start at the beginning…"

Mariah leans in toward him listening intently all the while twisting that favorite strand of hair.

CHAPTER EIGHT

Ted, the morgue attendant, slowly unzips the dark colored body bag. He listens as Doc tells him what to do, "OK Ted, let's move him. Careful." With Doc's help, Ted moves Jocko onto the autopsy table. "I'd like to take a look at the body again before we start, "Doc explains, "Just to see if I missed something before we brought him in."

Doc turns on his portable tape recorder. "Captain Jocko Compton, age 77, died of an apparent heart attack. Autopsy in progress because no attending physician present at the time of death."

"Judging by the levidity of the body, Jocko died right in the chair just the way he was found. Rigor mortis has set in. His eyes were wide open and his jaw dropped. My estimate is that our patient has been dead about 26-28 hours making the time of death between ten A.M. and twelve noon on August 9, 1986. Body temperature in the lab confirms the time. There are signs of vomiting and extreme diarrhea. His left arm shows signs of bruising and multiple needle marks. Looking at the physical condition of the body, there are thin red lines around sides of mouth. Multiple needle marks in his left arm appear larger than they normally might be."

"There is mild bruising around his right wrist. Patient, a diabetic, is on insulin. I will now proceed with the blood work." Doc shuts off the tape recorder and looks over at the small observation room. "Bill, we should have those results sometime today. I'll put a rush on it."

Doc slowly looks at the Captain. "I think we caught everything. OK Ted, you can prepare the body for autopsy."

"I'm on top of it Doc, I'll get him ready." With that, Ted begins to undress the captain and clean his body in preparation for the invasive medical post mortem examination. Jocko's clothes and personal things are carefully bagged and coded before being sent off to the lab for any traces of deadly substances. This procedure takes a little longer than unusual as there are only two people working on the situation. Ted has assisted before, but this is Doc's one and only post mortem.

Once the body is ready, Doc starts his examination. He instructs the young attendant,

"Wait for me to complete all of the blood and bodily fluid tests before taking them to the lab. We need the full results ASAP"

"I'm on it Doc," Ted retorts.

Doc doesn't really hear Ted because he is immersed in his own dilemma, "I hope I get through this without vomiting all over Jocko." Doc draws the Captain's blood and gathers body fluids necessary to determine the cause of death.

Bill watches as the flow of deep magenta, clear and yellowish fluids fill the clear tubes.

Doc further instructs Ted, "I want these checked for any abnormal substances, bacteria, drugs, etc in his blood, ASAP."

The attendant goes over to the wall phone to call the lab for a pickup. Once that's done, Ted hears Doc's voice again. "O.K. let's continue," Doc says as he turns the tape recorder on.

"I am about to open the chest cavity."

Doc picks up the drill like instrument, turns it on to a whirring buzz and starts to make the incision. Blood spatters all over them, Bill takes one look, turns very pale, and passes out cold.

Doc stops the procedure and clicks off the recorder not wanting to embarrass Bill.

"Bill are you with us? Ted hurry, go over there and help him." Doc chuckles as Ted runs into the booth and administers smelling salts. Bill comes to a bit surprised at what just happened.

"Ted,' Doc says without looking up, "Call the lab again. Tell them we need a pick up now. Tell them we'll keep calling every ten minutes until they show up. Tell them that the fluids may be evidence in a murder case. Oh and remind them to be as thorough and careful as possible."

As Ted goes to the phone, Doc quickly turns on the recorder, places it close by and continues to speak. "I have finished the incision and am pulling the layers of skin apart to examine the chest cavity more closely."

He then places his hands in the chest cavity again and pulls out Jocko's heart. He holds it up slowly examining the arteries while looking for any signs of damage. He looks very closely at its condition and then weighs it.

"All aspect's of the heart's condition suggests that the patient died from sudden congestive heart failure. There is evidence of tachycardia putting stress on the heart and causing atrioventricular blockage. As his primary physician, I have to admit I saw no symptoms of this in any exam or tests prior to his demise. I just gave him his yearly physical about a month ago and his heart tested to be in good shape. I find this to be more than a bit odd though it may not be totally unusual. I'd like to note again that the patient was a diabetic. I will now examine the stomach and kidneys."

Doc continues with the exam. Bill, still a bit pale, looks in from the glass enclosure. He is nodding his head in agreement. Bill remains calm by the fact that both Doc and Ted display such a strong sense of responsibility and respect for his job as a police investigator. This is not, however, how Bill has seen Ted act outside of the hospital.

Bill's mind wanders a bit relieving some of his stress. He looks at Ted.

"Boy, Ted sure is different at work. He is one strange dude in Mariah's store. He's there every single day. For a guy that works in the morgue you'd think he's seen enough of the dead. But no, he rents old supernatural thrillers."

"I still remember the look on Mariah's face the day Ted told her that he is part dog. Part dog. I almost choked on that one. He actually believes that one of his ancient ancestors mated with an alpha male. Because of this, Ted believes he inherited his natural spirituality and psychic abilities. Oh well, he's original. I'll give him that much."

"Ted then told Mariah that he's a pet communicator. There's the real reason he likes the video store so much, Spike. It's all a bunch of hooey, but I still watch every single time as he holds Spike's head in his hands and stares into his eyes. Good thing Spike is good-natured. I would bite the guy. The two appear as if they're relaying images back and forth sort of like alien transmissions. Ted blinks and then begins to reveal Spike's innermost thoughts."

Bill hears another unpleasant noise; his mind suddenly snaps back to the present. "Damn, I can't believe that Ted actually works here. Wonder if he talks to the corpses too."

Bill laughs to himself but regains his composure as his eyes shift back to Doc. Doc is examining and weighing the lungs. Doc then proceeds with the rest of the exam.

Bill hears the dreaded loud and piercing sound of the drill again. He forces himself to watch as the rest of Jocko's organs are identified, weighed and examined. Bill is quietly glad to observe from the glass observation room. He doesn't think the fluids and smells would agree with him. At last, he hears Doc describe the old guys last meal." OK, Bill, this should wrap up the exam."

Bill nods his head as he sways back and forth. "Wonder how Mariah's holding up?" With those thoughts, he literally passes out again. The stress is too much. Lucky for him, a very pretty female assistant within earshot comes to help revive the handsome deputy in uniform. Bill should know better than to worry about Mariah. She's always been a tough cracker very capable of taking care of herself.

Doc begins to sew Jocko up with Ted's assistance.

For someone who was so anxious to proceed with Jocko's autopsy, Bill is just as relieved as Doc that it's finally over. His face still carries a gray pallor.

What seems like an eternity for two of the three men has finally reached a conclusion. Each unbeknownst to the other breathes a silent sigh of relief simultaneously. Bill comes in from the observation room as Ted prepares to take the body back to storage.

"Well Bill," Doc advises," We've done as much as we can. We know now that Jocko's death was not caused by an injury, accidental or on purpose. We're left with unanswered questions about the condition of his heart. We will now have to wait for the toxicology reports to see what might have caused those funny marks on his arm. If he was poisoned, we need to know how and by what? We are left with questions that may lead to suspicious answers. I guess Jocko's death does merit investigating as a murder."

Doc looks at Ted. "O.K. Ted let's put Jocko away."

Ted rolls the gurney over to the cold stainless steel drawers and slides Jocko's body onto the long shelf. He closes the drawer,

"Bill," Doc continues, "I'll call you as soon as I hear something."

Bill nods, thanks Doc for his help, turns around to face the exit and heads for his cruiser.

Ted leaves the room as well.

Doc, sensing that there are no witnesses, collapses into the nearest chair relieved that he was able to complete the job expected of him without embarrassment.

"I can't believe it's over." Doc's heart is still pounding. "Boy, do I ever need a drink. Time to head for the Sandbarre."

Needless to say, The Sandbarre is Doc's favorite watering hole along with many other island locals. However, for good measure, medicinal reasons of course, and until he physically can get himself there.

Doc pulls a small sterling silver flask out of his pants pocket. Ironically, the flask was a gift from Jocko who had it monogrammed "Doc." He raises the flask in the air and salutes his fallen friend and then proceeds to gulp a big swig of some pretty expensive single malt scotch knowing full well that Jocko is looking down in complete approval.

He then gets himself up, shakes himself sane, and goes into the scrub room to shower and change.

CHAPTER NINE

"When you reach my age, time passes by too quickly," Pacco speaks pulling his shoulders back to straighten his posture so that he sits perfectly upright on the rattan barstool. "It seems like only yesterday when Senora Anna and the Captain met."

Pacco then places his arms on the counter, hands folded like he is about to discuss something of great importance. He stares into Mariah's eyes as he lifts one hand to pull on the ends of his finely groomed black mustache.

Mariah leans forward looking him directly at him with eager anticipation.

"Senorita, I can tell you care about the Captain. I have worked for Senor Jocko and Senora Anna for many years. I care for both of them as well." Pacco's hands begin to waive in the air with gestures as he begins;

"Together they own a pottery factory in Ojuana."

"Ojuana? Where is Ojuana?" A curious Mariah asks.

"It is on the Gulf side across from Florida. That location makes it easy for Senor Jocko to go back and forth. He and Anna met there twenty-six years ago. She was and is beautiful in my country's tradition. When they met, Senora Anna was young, maybe eighteen. They have been in love for many years. Senora Anna had no money so Captain Jocko started a pottery factory for her in Ojuana. Senora Anna loves to paint the pots and does such beautiful work that her pots sell all over Mexico. Captain Jocko thinks it a good business for her to have. So he buys a small, how do you say, hard concreta building."

"Concrete?" Mariah interjects,

"Si concrete building right in the center of town. That way it is easy to find workers. Everyone loves them both so much that the people line up in hopes of working for them."

Mariah's interest is now piqued by Pacco's every word.

"You refer to Anna as Senora. Were they married there?"

Pacco looks at Mariah, "No, They have been together so long it is as if they are married. We all call her Senora as a sign of respect."

Mariah cannot stop with her questions, "How long would Jocko stay in Ojuana?"

"Well, he would come for a few months for a rest from shrimping and then he would return to Florida. Senora Anna could run the business by herself. She had good men like me working there who showed their respect for both of them. I would watch out for her."

"How big was or is the factory? Is it still open?"

Mariah watches as Pacco's eyes work the room as if searching for something special again, She interrupts his wandering eyes with another question,

"When was the last time you saw or spoke to Jocko? Were you both here or in Ojuana?"

Pacco's eyes abruptly shift back to Mariah's. "The last time I saw Senior Jocko was two days ago. I want to help him get ready for the trip home to Ojuana. He would send me to the grocery or help him clean up here. He wanted me to get supplies for the sea trip home." Pacco stops and lights up another cigarette. Mariah automatically pushes over the ashtray.

"Jocko hates me to smoke. I have to be very very careful never to get smoke near him; He would never let me smoke here. The Captain is" Pacco catches himself "was a neat man. Not only here but also in Ojuana. Factory always has to be kept just so."

Pacco carefully flicks the cigarette ashes into the ashtray. Mariah looks at it hoping to retrieve pirate's treasure when he leaves.

"The last day I saw him was here. He asked me to bring him dinner. I made something special for him. I asked me when I came if he wants me to return the movie. He said no. He wanted to watch it to the end so I leave it here for him."

Mariah is still listening intently. "You helped him a great deal and must know his apartment well."

Pacco nods his head "Si."

Mariah continues, "When you were here last, did you notice if the back doors were left unlocked? Do you remember any mess, cigarette ashes or anything else that might seem unusual?' Mariah is pretty proud of her last question.

Pacco pauses for a minute as if thinking and then responds,

"No Senorita, no doors open. Captain Jocko would not be happy if all the cold air go out the back. I have never found a mess because, as I say, Senior Jocko is very neat."

Pacco's black beady eyes search the room one more time. Once again by his expression Mariah could tell that his search found nothing. Mariah's head turns to follow Pacco's gaze but this proves to be a big mistake. As she looks away, the savvy old gentleman empties his cigarette ashes as well as the ashtray into his pocket. He then gets up from the barstool rather abruptly.

Mariah's eyes revert back to him. As he gets up, he tells her, "I must go now to call Senora Anna. She will want Jocko to be buried in Ojuana. Goodbye." He nods his head as if almost bowing.

Pacco then lifts the yellow crime scene tape and leaves the apartment the exact way he came. Mariah notices the missing ashtray.

She stares at the counter, speechless at her own stupidity.

"He's gone...vanished as quickly as he came. Worse yet," Mariah thinks, "There are now no ashes or cigarette butts to prove that he was even here or to match with the ones we found. Now there's only my word."

"Well Spike, I guess I'm not as sharp as I'd like to think I am. Pacco sure has nothing to worry about, hey old boy?"

Spike loves the sound of Mariah's voice. He tilts his head from side to the side lifting his ears whenever she speaks to him.

Mariah believes that very few people in her life actually do listen to her, especially anyone who works for her. Spike genuinely makes her feel good. Mariah begins to gather her things realizing that she by now has overstayed her welcome.

"Better get a move on Spike before we are caught in here red handed."

She fastens Spike's leash, picks up her purse and heads toward the yellow tape when she stops short, startled by the fact that someone new is now standing in the doorway staring right at her.

A beautiful, tall, olive skinned middle-aged woman elegantly dressed in black and wearing a wide-brimmed black straw hat faces Mariah directly. The brim casts a shadow over her finely sculptured features. Even so, her large brown almond eyes catch Mariah's through the layers of netting. She opens her mouth to speak. Both Mariah and Spike are frozen speechless to say the least.

"My Jocko. Where is he?" The woman in black asks in tears.

CHAPTER TEN

If you were to peek through her window, Moonbeam always gives the impression of being busy, very busy. In reality, she's just cleaning up after her last and most puzzling client of the day.

She gently places her Oriental flowered china teapot and two delicate small round cups on a tray and takes them into the kitchen where she carefully washes them adding some frangipani-scented detergent to the water. This delicate yet sweet floral scent when sprayed in the reading room works magic with the rich herbal teas; inhaled, it can transport even the most stressed client into a state of total relaxation. Moonbeam soaks in their fragrances, "Oh how wonderfully sweet the air is! Thank you my beautiful flowers and tea for enchanting my clients. You make them totally relaxed under your spell. You lift them to a different plane; one of softness, friendship and calmness."

Moonbeam knows the importance of atmosphere. After all, she moved to Seabliss from the cold winds of Chicago six years ago. She has never regretted her change of atmosphere.

Her real name is Julia Mooreham and she had previously worked as an accountant in a commodities trading firm. The stress of her job finally reached its peak. She has always been fascinated with the occult, taking courses and testing her own psychic strength with others who "possessed" the gift. Now known as Moonbeam, she cares deeply about matters of the spirit. For Julia, moving to Seabliss gave her a chance to start over in life and reinvent herself. Many other transplants on the island changed the direction of their lives as well for one reason or another, maybe finances, maybe divorce, or maybe just to hide from the law.

Now in her mid thirties, she is still very attractive in an exotic way. She wears her long blond curly hair tied back with brightly colored Jamaican bandanas. Her light bronze eyes are the color of a lion's at sunset. She loves to wear so many silver ankle bracelets that her walk turns her into a human wind chime. Wearing long light pastel patterned skirts with strapless halter-tops, Moonbeam's choice of clothes has become her trademark and she can usually be found barefoot. Strands of silver chains adorn her neck; each chain holding a significant crystal with powers that protect both her mind and body from all sorts of evil. When someone admires one of her chains, Moonbeam identifies that crystal. She literally takes the necklace off and sells it to the person.

Once at home, she then replaces it with another from the inventory in her back "office." She rents videos from Mariah's store. Because of this, they have become close buddies often laughing about who will win their worst customer of the day contest.

Wiping her teapot dry, Moonbeam can hear someone coming up the two lavender concrete front steps to her front door. She looks out her window and sees Doc happily bouncing up the stairs.

"Hello my love, I have just had one of the worst days of my medical career and I want to whisk you off to the Sandbarre for afternoon cocktails that may extend well into the evening."

"Hey Doc, I'm on. My last client messed my head up more than I did hers."f Hang on a second. I'll grab my purse."

Moonbeam walks over to Doc and gives him a quick kiss on the cheek.

She grabs her red and pink beaded shoulder bag from the hall tree. She turns and touches his shoulder.

"Let's go Babe, I'll share my horror story if you share yours."

Moonbeam locks the peach wooden front door with a crescent moon and stars painted on it.

The two walk a few blocks to the island's square where they enter the Sandbarre, the local watering hole, noted for its beautiful gulf front views, sunsets, friendly staff and conch fritters that are to die for.

Both beat from the day's stress, Doc and Moonbeam quietly walk through the shell arch that leads to the outside bar area. They are a very popular island couple often sought after for parties. As they walk by the other tables, they are greeted by the smiles and nods of the many familiar faces of local residents who acknowledge them as they pass.

"Hey Doc Hey Moonie how's things?" Lizzie their favorite server greets them

"Well, I wish I could say great but 'unusual' would sum up today for me."

Doc answers

"Me too" Moonbeam chimes in "and now we're prepared to drown our sorrows."

They find a table where they can look out at the water and still remain private. There they sit quietly for a few minutes holding hands and looking at the beach. Doc soon signals for Lizzie to come over.

Lizzie has served them so often that she can write their order without being told; she's polite and listens nonetheless. Doc orders, "Hey, Lizzie, I'll have my usual Glenfiddich on the rocks, while for my lovely lady, I'll order a Bacardi and coke with lime." The drinks arrive quickly as do a bowl of peanuts in the shells. Lizzie leaves right away sensing their need for privacy.

"Doc, honey you look beat. Tell me what happened." Moonbeam looks at her lover sympathetically.

"I should be a comedian and remind you that you should know already considering your chosen line of work. But I'll be nice and not give you all of the gory details. This is a concise accounting of the day's events. As you probably know by now, poor Jocko died. Mariah found him and called the police. Everything appeared normal until she started playing detective convincing Bill that there might be fowl play. So you know what that means, Jocko would have to have an autopsy. Since the M.E. and assistant M.E. are out of town and I'm covering as a favor and the autopsy can't wait…"

"I did hear about Jocko. I'm so sad. Oh, You poor dear," Moonbeam interrupts, "You had to cut up Jocko."

"Well, you sure don't mince your words," Doc blurts out.

"Did you find anything suspicious?" Moonbeam hopes to get some new information for Mariah. "You know, come to think of it, I've been having bad dreams for the past two nights as if an old spirit wanted to contact me from beyond the grave. The spirit is male and knows my name…" Moonbeam closes her eyes and lifts her arms in the air as if trying to make contact.

"Save it for your fans, sweetie," Doc responds with a smile, "The answer to your question is yes and maybe." Everything looked pretty normal except for some unusual vein marks with discoloration and some purplish lines and dried vomit around the mouth. I'm waiting for the lab reports on both the bodily fluids and on Jocko's clothes."

Doc continues, "I have absolutely no idea what Spike and Mariah were doing there. I'm sure there's a good explanation. Lucky she was because

Jocko would have been like that for days living alone the way he did."

"Poor man," Moonbeams sighs, "Poor Mariah. Jocko was like a father to her. She must be beside herself with grief."

"Well" Doc interjects, "Enough sad news. Let's move on to the unusual and bizarre. How was your day my sweet soothsayer? Let's have all the dish…" Doc takes a big gulp of his scotch.

"I don't know if it's dish or bizarre. A very beautiful well dressed woman with long dark braided hair wearing a black veiled hat stopped by for me to tell her fortune. She spoke in broken English. I think that she's Spanish. She asked me some rather strange questions." Moonbeam pauses for a minute and shelled a peanut to munch.

"O.K," Doc interjects, "You got me hooked. Besides right about now, I need a good laugh. What did she ask that you of all people would find strange?"

"She asked if tiny crystals could really bring happiness to her life as promised and if a tall man will cross the sea?"

Doc sits back in his chair and smiles "You do meet some strange ones. How did you handle her?"

"I just answered 'Yes' to both guessing that that's the answer she wanted to hear. Otherwise, why would she ask me those specific questions?"

Moonbeam is pretty proud of herself; her two undergraduate years of psychology are finally paying off.

Doc looks at her warmly, "Very perceptive my dear and I imagine you answered solemnly."

Moonbeam smiles "Oh yes, I held her hand and looked into her eyes as best I could with her veil on and said slowly Yes my dear, your anticipations shall be fulfilled."

"She seemed happy at that response and paid me one hundred and fifty dollars for the emergency visit."

"Maybe you should buy the drinks," Doc laughs.

Moonbeam is not laughing at his remark. Doc smiles until his pager goes off.

"Uh, oh got to run. It's the lab; they must've found something. I promised Bill I would let him know ASAP."

With that, Doc gets up from the chair, finishes his drink, and leaves Moonbeam alone to finish hers and pick up the tab.

CHAPTER ELEVEN

"I need to know, where my Jocko is?" The mysterious woman in the doorway repeats her question as she takes a deep breath. She appears to be nervous but not nearly as nervous as Mariah.

Mariah just looks at her not knowing how or where to begin. "I'm so very sorry to have to be the one to tell you this. Jocko was found dead this morning. He was taken to the county morgue."

The woman collapses falling to her knees. She places her hand over her veiled mouth to silence her deep sobs. Spike starts to whimper in sympathy at the sound of her crying. Mariah is trying to distinguish her facial features but it is difficult considering that the woman's head is tilted downward and she is wearing a wide brimmed veiled black hat.

"I'm truly sorry Ma'am. I am a friend of Jocko's too."

"I know who you are," the woman responds looking up, "You're Mariah. Jocko has mentioned you a great deal to me."

Mariah, taken by surprise, thinks, "So this must be the mystical Anna."

She walks over to the woman and helps her to her feet. "Please come over to the kitchen counter and sit down until you feel better. We can't stay in here too much longer. The police chief won't allow it"

The woman stands up and walks the short distance to the counter stool. She sits down and lifts the veil to her hat.

Mariah studies her features. She is beautiful with facial features that appear to have been sculpted like those of a classical statue. Her black dress is simple; her long dark hair braided tightly back underneath her hat. She wears an elaborate heavy silver necklace of carved wildflowers with emerald centers. Anna, who appears to be in her mid forties, possesses the kind of beauty that is ageless.

Mariah is savvy enough not refer to Anna by name. After all, she would not want Anna to think that she had been prying by reading Jocko's most private letters.

As Anna regains her composure, she begins to ask questions about Jocko's death.

"Were others from the village here to see him? I tried to warn Jocko about them. They threatened to do bad things to him if he did not sell his shares of our business."

Mariah remembers some of the things that she read but cannot speak about them.

"Who are these people? Jocko never mentioned them or you to me. He told me he was just a retired sea captain."

The woman smiles faintly, "Forgive me my dear, my name is Anna. I have loved Jocko for many years. We work together in our small Mexican village where Jocko stayed after coming for a holiday. We have a pottery factory."

Mariah sits back on the barstool. Her mind works overtime, "I'm confused. Jocko was supposed to be retired. Now I find out he has a lover, a factory, and a gang of evil people who threatened him. I wonder what else I should know?"

Anna answers as if reading her mind.

"Well my dear, you must know that his ex-wife lives in this same building. I used to be jealous but Jocko said he just wanted to make sure she is cared for properly. I guess her new husband, a man named Taggert, used to compete with Jocko for cargo and has a bad temper."

By now, Mariah could feel her jaw drop so low she wonders if her tonsils show. She is once again taken by complete surprise. "I know Taggert, but quite honestly, Jocko never mentioned anything about his ex-wife or his past connection to Taggert."

"All I know," Mariah continues, "Is that I will miss Jocko dearly. He's been like a second father to me and so kind to Spike."

Tears stream down Anna's face, "And so will I. He was the love of my life."

The two women get up and console each other with a hug. Anna tells Mariah, "I am staying at The Blue Heron Inn. If I can be of any assistance, please do not hesitate to contact me."

Mariah nods and then escorts Anna to the door. She turns the lock on the doorknob from the inside as the two women leave Jocko's apartment together slowly. Spike follows with a heavy tail weighed down by the sorrow he can feel coming from his master's heart.

CHAPTER TWELVE
JOCKO'S OTHER LIFE

Long before Jocko's life ended so abruptly, he was the envy of many of his fellow sea captains.

They envied his lifestyle, his love, and his apparent lack of fear of drug dealers and pirates.

"Ojuana is more than a homeport; it's a hidden gem," he would often brag to the other captains. "Lucky for me, it remains undiscovered by tourists. I made a promise to Anna and my workers that I would try to keep it pure of criminals."

It's no wonder Jocko felt that way. This quaint little fishing village has streets lined with rows of faded pastel concrete cottages. The main cobblestone street leading to the center of town is bordered with bright pink, lavender and coral hibiscus and bougainvillea.

"Whenever I go to town,' Jocko would continue, "I enjoy watching the young children dressed in light clothing play hide and seek and tag in the street. The best part of my walk comes when I turn around and look down the hill to see my queen, the magnificent Gulf of Mexico."

Jocko loved the fact that Ojuana's white sand beaches are surrounded by lush tropical jungle. The jungle adds a breath of coolness to an area that parches in the extreme of bright sunlight. Small fishing boats bob in the waters not far from shore. Bronzed men work their nets hoping to bring home a catch worth selling or at least worth having for their family's dinner.

A whitewashed old Spanish mission stands tall as the town's magnificent centerpiece. Draped with hanging vines of purplish pink flowers, the mission has an old bell tower, and a courtyard that contains the village cemetery. The Padre, Father Florentino, has taken care of this mission for a long time, having baptized, married or buried many residents of Ojuana.

Inside, the mission boasts beautifully painted frescos from the seventeen hundreds by artists who were brought over from Spain during Mexico's colonial days. It is there that the elders of the town meet protected from the sun's rays almost daily to reminisce about family histories and stories from the past. The elders are as much a treasure as the paintings for all who worship there.

Anna and Jocko's pottery factory is also located in the center of town not too far down the road from the mission. One just has to walk by a little grocery store and fruit stand, a bar and restaurant, the only entertainment in town, to arrive at the factory's front door.

The factory building displays a faded exterior of tan stucco with many of the walls in need of repair. Graffiti and spontaneous paintings cover one side of the exterior; there are no glass or screened windows just open spaces cut out for air and light. The openings have metal slant shutters with cranks that will close for cover during the torrential and fast paced rainstorms. Of course, there is no air conditioning at the factory but the employees do not seem to mind. They are used to the heat since their houses are not air-conditioned either.

For the locals, work at the factory is steady and Anna and Jocko treat them well. The factory consists of two large open rooms and a very small one that Anna uses as an office. The first area serves as a showroom where customers and buyers from the bigger cities enter to view the new pieces. There is a desk for orders and an area where the buyers can watch the local women seated at workbenches painting the pots, urns and figurines. The back room is equally as big and houses the kilns.

The women, especially Anna, hand paint each piece of pottery with bright colors and beautiful designs. The village men are equally proud as they man the kilns. Anna's pottery is so beautiful that many owners of tourist gift shops in Cancun and Cozumel travel hours to load up their trucks or boats in order to sell these pots in their shops. "Pots By Anna "has become a very popular brand throughout the Gulf Coast Mexican vacation spots.

Anna and Jocko's workers, grateful for an alternative job to fishing, are happy with their lives; they love to spend Sundays at the parish yard sharing family picnics. They are rich in spirit; they know they could make much more money assisting the drug lord Luis but remain content to take pride in honest work to support their families. Some of the younger residents travel to Florida during the winter months to work in hotels and restaurants so that they can send money home to their older relatives. Life in Ojuana is poor but not pathetic.

There is enough to eat, to pay their small bills and enough time off. It would seem idyllic, except for the fact that Luis and his men live in a compound on a hill not too far out of town.

Unfortunately, the most lucrative jobs in Ojuana are not at Anna's factory. The richest residents work at dealing in drugs. They smuggle and traffic for the notorious Luis.

Luis' Spanish style compound hangs over the small village like a threatening storm cloud. The villa is beautiful with all of its massive front windows having spectacular Gulf views. The house is large with a sprawling floor plan. The Olympic swimming pool is adorned with life sized authentic Greek statues Luis purchased on the hushed but sizable antiquities black market. Luis had these incredible finds shipped directly to Ojuana from his visit to Delos, in the Greek islands.

The main building has two floors; the first floor is used as a guardroom where Luis' men can monitor the hundreds of surveillance cameras that cover the perimeters of the property as well as all the entrances to the compound. Luis has his men watch those monitors twenty four seven for unwanted visitors especially any from his jealous competitors.

Any time Luis' security team sees something suspicious, they alert the armed guards who will stop and detain any visitor, sometimes for good.

Tall concrete walls housing the cameras surround the property; an ornate heavy old wrought iron gate serves as a physical and as well as a visual deterrent. Luis is proud of himself for having found this elaborate gate at the estate sale of Spanish Royalty. The black gate serves as stark contrast to the whitewashed concrete walls. He paid handsomely to have it shipped home. For Luis, money has never been a problem.

The upstairs residence is quite elegant reflecting a Mediterranean style with white stucco walls, dark woodwork, and mahogany furniture, very Spanish indeed. Luis' collection of fine art adorns the walls and is worth millions. Considering his line of work, Luis believes it best to invest his illegal cash in untraceable but highly saleable items like antiques, jewels, and paintings.

Noted as the most feared drug trafficker in this coastal region of Mexico, Luis selected Ojuana for his hub because of its remoteness and its non-commercial port ideal for direct shipping to the states. There is one other major player in the area, a competitor named Juan Blanco, who works farther to the

North, but Luis has already informed him that he will not attend his young daughter's wedding if he interferes with Luis' business.

Sophisticated and savvy, Luis wears only the most expensive custom suits from Italy, silk French ties, Spanish shoes and designer sunglasses. Physically, he appears to have a constant tan. His face is smooth and well shaven. His jet-black hair is short and combed back showcasing his chiseled nose and aristocratic features. He looks younger than his forty-eight years and is very muscular. Luis keeps himself in shape with martial arts training. His home gym rivals any public one and of course he uses his hilltop pool and Jacuzzi daily.

To say that Luis is very popular with women is an understatement. He has been linked romantically with many beautiful and rich women in Mexico, Florida and Spain. Heads turn whenever he enters a room. Luis could easily pass for royalty except for one feature, a shiny gold cap on the left side of his smile. It sparkles ominously in the sunshine becoming his mark of distinction.

In spite of his gold tooth, most women are happy to throw themselves at his feet. The one exception is the woman he wants most. Her name is Anna. Jocko's Anna is the one that Luis would love to love. "Anna" has a natural beauty. She is very smart with a good business sense. Oh, she would be perfect for me. I will make her come to her senses by whatever means possible. I want to spoil her with romantic trips to Paris and a life filled with luxury. I will change her mind about me. I would do anything for her, but so far, she wants nothing to do with me."

Luis has tried some heavy-handed methods of persuasion, raiding her business hoping to scare her into submission. Anna knows that much of Luis' interest in her centers on using her factory as a front for shipping drugs. She remembers how Luis used to export his drugs through a local's seasoning plant. Luis' competitors burned it down shooting his manager in the head. Anna doesn't know that he really does love her. He truly does and will not give up until she returns his affection. "Our merger, " Luis often thinks, "would be unstoppable."

CHAPTER THIRTEEN
ANNA'S WARNING

Anna, on the other hand, does not share Luis' affection. She is embarrassed and sometimes even frightened by Luis' open and public display of his romantic interest in her. He's never been shy about displaying his affection. After all, a man like Luis always gets what he wants.

Anna knows, "I must maintain my integrity. I must fight him off every chance I get. I want no part of how he earns his evil money. I don't want to see my small pottery factory become the highly profitable core of his drug dealing. I'm afraid that he wants my plant as badly as he wants my body. What happens when I'm old and no longer desirable? Will he kill me as he has done many of the other women who sooner or later bore him?"

"My factory is small and somewhat primitive, but it makes enough profit to earn a decent living. I'm pleased that I can now help Jocko in his retirement. After all, he helped me when I had nothing. His love is steady and sure. I'm proud of us and the business we built together."

Anna is pleased that her pots are so popular. Her latest sales have increased her bottom line even more. Recently, she started shipping to the US on local fishing boats she knows are clean of drugs. "If I don't hire the boats wisely, all of my hard work will be destroyed by customs officials eager to search for illegal goods."

"I wish I knew how to stop Luis. He doesn't take 'no' lightly. He insists on showering me with long stemmed red roses. One day, he sent so many floral arrangements to my plant that I couldn't get into my office."

Anna's office is cramped but colorful. Even with its primitive concrete walls, it carries an artistic feel.

The walls are painted in the bright primary colors of yellow and bright blue. Cheerful pottery decorated with red and pink tropical flowers fill wall shelves behind her old carved wooden desk. There is a window to the inside of the plant so that she can always monitor what is going on. The outside wall has a window with slats that open to the small village. She has placed window boxes on them filled with white and pink geraniums. Embroidered white cotton curtains with flowers that match the colors of the room grace the outside windows and gently move with the tropical breeze. Unfortunately, there is no alarm system. Luis is very aware of this and uses it to his advantage. He remains determined to win her over realizing that he has the edge on Jocko in money and men.

She has often told Jocko about Luis' advances. "I get so angry just thinking that he believes that he can buy my affection with expensive jewelry and perfume. I send everything back but it only seems to only make Luis want me more."

She makes it perfectly clear time after time that she will have nothing to do with him. He refuses to give up.

A few months prior to Jocko's death, Luis, determined to change Anna's mind, tries to bribe some of her key workmen. He tells them, "I'll pay you large bonuses, give your families extra groceries, tequila and clothes. Name your price. Everyone has one. I just might surprise you by paying it."

So far, Anna has been very lucky, always able to nip the newest crisis in the bud by firing the traitor of the day and setting an example of him in front of the other workers before they too are led astray.

When his acts of "kindness" fail, he sends in his thugs. On this one day, Luis calls, "Enrico and Roberto, my two loyal guard dogs, Go to Anna's plant to change her workers' minds by whatever means necessary. Jump on the worktables, destroy their daily work, and threaten to burn the place down. Make a scene they'll remember, but don't hurt anyone this time. Let them feel the power of Luis and show them how afraid Anna is of me. Give her this note from me without being noticed. Then leave as quickly as you came."

The pair drive over to the plant in their old faded blue Ford Fairlane. They smile seeing that the plant is open and full of workers. The two thugs get out of the car; slamming the car doors shut so that anyone within earshot will realize that they have arrived. They approach the front door kicking it open. With their guns held up in the air for all to see, they fire a warning shot at the ceiling. Plaster falls like snow.

The workers begin to panic as they witness Enrico jump on a graying wooden worktable. Roberto remains on the floor throwing pots to the ground smashing them to bits. They men shelter the frightened women in their arms.

There is sobbing and cries of "Stop, please stop!" Enrico has heard enough. He fires his gun at the ceiling one more time. "We'll be back to burn this rubble of a place down if Miss Anna does not heed the warnings of the great Luis. Do you all understand?" The workers shake their already shaking heads "Yes." Enrico gets down and with Roberto heads for the door. Before leaving they quickly hand off the note to Anna from Luis.

Anna is horrified as she watches the thugs kick some of the broken pots around on their way out. Anna holds back her tears. A day's worth of work is destroyed. Her workers feel very insecure and hurt. Trembling, she climbs up on the same table that Enrico stood on. Showing courage, she tells her workers,

"Please don't let these thugs get to you. I'm not going to give into them and neither will you. Once we do that, they win. We'll now clean up and go back to work. I intend to send Luis a bill for all of his damage!"

The men begin to whisper, "I know that they'll be back. What will do we do the next time?" Anna sensing this quickly announces,

"I will hire security guards to watch over us and protect our work. I'll not let this happen again! Stay calm…Go back to your work. We will get through this together as a family."

Her speech is greeted with mixed responses. Juan Carlos and his cousin nod their head, "We stand behind you, Anna. We stand behind you." But not all agree. Fredo raises his fist and with five others decides to leave, "We're afraid. We're done. We quit. We know that Luis will be more violent the next time and there will be a next time. Luis is not stupid enough to burn down something he needs so desperately. He might, however, kill us all as we are expendable to him."

Juan Carlos holds his ground, "Remember people, Anna gives us work, honest work. Jocko helps our families. We cannot turn our back on her now, can we?" Anna is relieved to hear more "No's" than "Yes."

The remaining employees all take deep breaths, pick up brooms and start to sweep up the debris. Using small dustpans, they sweep the clay pieces into big trash barrels. The cleaning process is slow but meticulous; by tomorrow they can return to work. At least Luis' men did not damage the equipment and they can be thankful for that.

Anna watches them from the open window in her office. She tries to calm down by telling herself,

"Today's fight brings a small victory for me. I know that we win every day my factory is open." She shouts courageously "Gracias Amigos" to her workers and raises her hands in applause. Everyone smiles and appears to react as if life is back to normal. Is it really or will the contents of the envelope that Enrico gave Anna pull her down a dark path? While the workers remain busy, she turns so she faces the outside window and opens the envelope from Luis.

"I must not read Luis' note at my desk. My workers can easily see what I do."

She turns her chair so she faces the street. As she unfolds the note, she can't stop her hands from trembling. She holds her stomach. She knows from the method of Luis' delivery that this message is of the gravest concern. She fumbles with the paper as her eyes follow the flowing Spanish handwriting:

"My Dearest Anna,

My love for you is strong. My respect for your business is sincere. I cannot tolerate the humiliation you have inflicted on me. You will inform Jocko today that I will buy out his shares of the factory and that I will make it worth his while. You and I can share my dream of building a life and business together. You will have millions of dollars at your disposal and live like a queen. I can assure you of that my beautiful Anna. Anything you want will be yours. You must obey these wishes or Jocko will not be able to decide his own future. You will make me decide his fate as well as yours. I will await your response. You have three days to answer. Tell Jocko he will be paid in cash for his trouble and you will be rewarded for a lifetime.

Yours forever in love,

Luis"

Anna's hands are still trembling. Stunned, she folds up the note as quickly as she can and puts it in her pocket.

"I have to leave work calmly without arising any suspicion." She stands and casually stretches and then goes back to her desk. Aware that she can be watched, she picks up the daily mail and a kerchief and prepares to leave as if she is going to the post box.

She looks out her office window into the plant. The workers are less stressed and back to work. They are cleaning up the debris, bagging the trash, and restoring workstations to their normal conditions. The local women who paint the beautiful and colorful designs have just arrived ready for work. The men and women on duty discuss the events of the day without making a big deal. Anna notices that some are taking a break and even laughing.

"I'm glad that they can still laugh," she thinks "Today has been a terrible day for all of us." She then peers quickly to the outside.

"No big men in black suits... Now, that's a good sign."

"I must try to make it to make it to the pay phone outside of Juan's Pub. I have to reach Jocko. He is in grave danger. I can't call from here. They can hear me. Besides I don't know who Luis has working on his payroll today. I must go and go quickly..."

Anna ties her kerchief, puts on a brave smile and reaches for the mail. She walks out calmly and slowly holding the mail so as it can be seen as she passes her workers. She gives each of them a squeeze on the shoulder or a pat on the back.

"I am so very proud of all of you!"

"Tomorrow is a new day!"

Her calmness permeates the plant making everyone settle down to his or her own tasks.

"If they only knew how big the knots are in my stomach. My only goal right now is to phone Jocko."

She has tied the kerchief so that it covers her sculptured profile, one that is easily recognizable by Luis. She leaves without suspicion. She steps out to the front step looks both ways for Luis' men and then starts briskly down the dirt road to Juan's.

Anna adjusts the silk scarf to cover more of her face. She does not want local well-wishers to stop and chat. She is on a mission, determined to warn Jocko. Juan's is three blocks from the plant. Anna walks briskly passing the many colorful cement cottages. Juan's handmade sign starts to become visible to Anna as she turns the corner. She knows that the phone booth is old and covered with graffiti but it works and that's all that counts right now. Once again, she looks across the street and behind her for Luis' men. As she reaches the phone booth she glances over at the open-air tavern. The phone booth is attached to a small building near an alley to the side of Juan's tavern.

She glances down that alley.

"I'm O.K.," she thinks picking up the receiver and dialing "O." Jocko always wants her to call collect.

"This is the operator. What number are you calling?" Anna gives her the information and soon hears his phone ring. Her hands are shaking so badly that the receiver is trembling. It shakes so much it distracts her ability to hear. She has to repeat the number twice. She hears Jocko's phone ringing again. The four short rings seem like forever to her. She then hears the operator ask

"Will you accept a collect call from Anna?"

"Yes" Anna is relieved to hear Jocko's voice.

"Capt Jocko here"

"Jocko you must listen to me. Luis came by with his men to try and destroy the plant. He scared some of the workers enough to quit. We have a problem with him…a big problem."

There is silence on the other end. Jocko's voice is filled with concern. "Anna I'll come right now. I don't want you to suffer in any way because of that dirt bag Luis or because of my past business dealings.

I'll talk to him face to face and iron out everything. I'll bring the "little gator" to help."

Jocko reaches for "little gator," a large curved fishing knife with a wide blade about eighteen inches long and not to be ignored.

Anna pleads with him, "No Jocko No, It's too late to talk. He's threatened to harm you if you don't sell him your shares of the factory He wants to use the factory as a front for his cocaine shipping. Luis will stop now at nothing. His enemies burned his other front down and killed his manager. Today he sent Enrico and Roberto to terrorize our workers and destroy every piece of work we made so far today. I was terrified just terrified!"

Jocko tries to comfort Anna.

"Anna, listen to me. I'll send you money. Just tell me what you need. Don't worry about your losses. I'll help. I love you."

That is the one thing that Anna does know for sure. She can even hear his love for her in the anger that Jocko's feels for Luis.

"That bastard should be shot. I'll be glad to be the one to do it. The world would be a better place without him. When I was younger I faced off against tougher rogues than that cowardly Luis; he is out scaring women imagine that!"

Anna tries to explain her concern further.

"Jocko you don't understand. He has power in men and money. He gave me a letter.

He wants to buy you out. Trust me, this devil means business."

"Jocko I am really frightened. Not just for me but for you. If anything should happen to you I don't know what I'd do. How could I ever forgive myself? I don't want to lose you yet I want to protect you and protect the workers. The factory means nothing without your love."

Anna wipes away tears as she tells him,

"I have to sign the papers and so do you."

"No, No, you will do no such thing. Anna." Jocko tells her, I've fought off smugglers and mercenaries. I've met my share of serious threats always like a man. This is no exception. You will not sign. I will be fine. Understand?"

Anna is still in tears. "But Jocko" The Captain's voice is stern.

"Anna, That money grubbin' Luis is a land pirate. I'll tell him to get a real job and work like the rest of us."

Anna pleads, "Luis will hurt you I know this. He'll kill you."

Jocko sighs, "Anna I'm a betting man and I'm betting on you and me. I never have walked away from a fight. I'd rather go down with the ship. That evil scum of a man will neither hurt you nor take away the factory. I won't let him ruin our lives. Luis should keep in mind his father's fate before he even thinks of threatening me."

Anna realizes that she can't talk any sense to him. She hears someone approaching.

CHAPTER FOURTEEN

"I have to go. Someone is coming. Be careful my love. I'll do what you ask."

Anna hangs up quickly. She crosses the alley and looking across the street, sees a tall thin man dressed entirely in black. He stares directly at her; she can feel his gaze pierce through his dark glasses. She smiles at him, hoping he is just a visitor wanting to find a phone. By now her stomach is churning from all the day's stresses. She turns to walk down the dirt road that leads her home. Her workday has been long enough.

Still somewhat frazzled, she glances back to see that the mystery man does not stop to use the phone. Anna picks up her pace. "Is he following me? Luis has made me paranoid. That man seems to be getting closer with every step." She starts to walk faster, as does the man. She crosses the narrow cobblestone street. The man follows. She turns around quickly to see him going into the local grocery store. She stops and catches her breath. "I must be going crazy," she thinks. "Luis has managed to take control of my mind."

"I think I'll take the long way home. It's so much more relaxing and quiet. I need the extra time to calm myself down. Today has been filled with agony." Anna decides not to be guided by fear.

The route is familiar with narrow side streets and beautiful flowers. It seems like forever but Anna finally turns the corner of her dead-end street. The walk home now seems so calming and peaceful. She sighs as if a tremendous burden has been lifted from her shoulders. Suddenly, it starts to rain, a cloudburst with cool refreshing drops. Anna takes off her kerchief to let her long black hair feel the freshness of the raindrops.

As she approaches the white wrought iron gate to her small cottage, she notices that the gate is ajar. "That's funny. I never leave the gate open. I hope Rosa didn't get out." Rosa is Anna's baby, a big beautiful black lab she adopted as a puppy.

Anna opens the front door slowly. "Rosa, Rosa, where are you. I'm home."

She doesn't hear Rosa running to greet her. She cautiously begins to look around the room.

"Oh no. He was here. I must find my Rosa." Anna's calm frame of mind now turns to one of worry. She finds herself surrounded literally by dozens of vases filled with long stemmed roses. Her small living room becomes a jungle with flowers of all colors and varieties; some are pink, coral, yellow, some with mixed colors. She knows of only one person with enough money to spend it like this.

Anna is quickly relieved to hear Rosa barking. It sounds like she is playing in the bedroom.

"Thank goodness, she must have gotten in there and the door closed behind her. I'm so relieved that he didn't harm her." Anna works her way around the flowers to the bedroom door. She hesitates, and then opens it to see Rosa happily getting her chew toy. Anna's eyes quickly move to her wicker chair. There's a man's black raincoat and hat like the mystery man's draped over one arm. She feels a hot breath on the back of her neck as she hears an all too familiar voice.

She gasps. It's her worst nightmare. Luis has followed her home. She thinks quickly," It's futile to scream. No one can hear me. I must remain calm and just listen to this devil."

"He must have followed me to the phone and knows that I called Jocko. He came to kill me. Poor Rosa, she has to watch all of this. She loves me so much. What will she do without me? "Anna, fearing more for her dog more than herself, becomes silent, bows her head and she prays for forgiveness in preparation of her execution.

To her surprise, however, Luis grabs her from behind and covers her mouth with his hand. She starts to punch him anywhere she can on his body. He forcefully turns her around so that she faces him and pulls her close to his chest. He removes his trademark dark glasses and throws them to the ground. She stops hitting him. She's in a state of shock. "He is going to kill me now. I know it." She wants to cry but refrains. "I won't give him the satisfaction," she thinks.

To her surprise, his voice becomes very tender.

"Anna, I don't think you know how I really feel," with that statement Luis pulls her in tighter. His black eyes looks longingly into hers. Luis kisses her cheeks and then gently yet passionately moves to her lips. His kiss is a long lingering passionate one. A few minutes go by before either of them move. Anna, frozen with fear, is surprised by her feelings. She shudders at the thought that she liked the kiss. She has never felt the sparks and the fireworks that accompany the deep passion of a younger man. She senses that Luis is really in love with her. His lips finally let hers go.

"Anna, give me the chance to win your heart. I promise you, you'll not be sorry."

Anna looks into his dark eyes. She says nothing, not knowing exactly what to say. His eyes as well as his demeanor seem so sincere.

Luis releases his grip. Anna is relaxed for a brief minute. She is soon grabbed again and thrown down on the bed. Luis holds her so that her hands are immobile. His lips press hard against hers again. She closes her eyes as her heart races. She tries to fight off his advances and tries to free herself. She kicks and tries to roll around but Luis is too strong to fight. Is she really trying to fight off Luis's advances or perhaps is she fighting the thought that she may actually be attracted to him.

She finally stops and gives into his advances, sensing the pounding of his heart, feeling the sheer strength of his muscular torso.

Luis in a tender voice speaks again, "Oh, my beautiful Anna…At last we're alone, I've waited an eternity for this."

Before she can say anything, he kisses her trembling lips again. "You must be quiet my love" Luis advises her covering her mouth with his hand. "You must be quiet. I did not come to harm you." He goes on,

"My love for you is as deep as the sea. You must believe me I have never felt this way about any other woman. I want to share my life and my fortune with you."

Anna remains frozen. She hates everything Luis stands for yet there is something kind about him. He seems so vulnerable, so handsome.

She stops herself, "How could I ever fall in love with such a man?"

Luis interrupts her thoughts. He kisses her hand.

"Do not scream. Please. I'll tell you again. I'm not here to harm you."

He gently kisses lips her again. Anna knows that she despises him yet the tenderness and seeming sincerity of the kiss causes her to tingle. She can sense his passion as well as her own. It's a passion she does not share with Jocko.

The kiss soon becomes enjoyable for both of them. He kisses her again and gently kisses her nose, her cheeks, and her eyes.

"Look at how much your dog likes me," Luis says playfully." Take a lesson from her I can't be all bad."

Anna cannot help but smile. She has never seen Luis behave like this. He is so playful, so tender and so caring.

"OK, Luis I won't scream," she manages a smile, "Tell me why you're really here. Is it for my factory or me? I would like so much to believe you. But how can I after your thugs raided my plant, scared my workers and damaged my products? If that's not enough, you even threatened my partner's life."

"I will give you proof of my love," With that Luis pulls Anna toward him once more and holds her. He passionately kisses her unbuttoning her blouse. Anna cannot pull away. She is caught up in the heat of the moment. Luis lifts her skirt. She can feel his body on hers trembling eager to consummate his love. He caresses her and tenderly makes love to her.

"Anna, come home with me. Move into my house. You and Rosa can live like queens with servants and fancy clothes and jewels and of course," he adds with a smile," the best dog food money can buy. I will give you anything your heart desires. We can travel and share our love. Say yes, Anna, please say yes."

Anna's eyes are still closed from their passion. He swept her off her feet. She doesn't know whether to feel joy or shame.

She soon comes to her senses.

"And what if I say no. Will you rip my house apart?…Hurt my dog? What will you do? Kill me?"

"Anna, my silly Anna, if all I wanted was your factory you would already be dead by now. Luis doesn't fool around. You are the love of my life. My love for you is unfailing…my passion relentless. I need you to make my life complete."

Luis continues "I already have workers on my payroll in your place. They can kill you on a moment's notice and take over. Obviously that's not my plan."

Anna is stunned. Her mind cannot help but wonder, "Who are these workers? Luis must be bluffing but can I afford to take a chance?"

Her thoughts race to her factory but she is afraid to voice them.

"Anna, my love, and that statement you must believe. I must leave you to take care of business. I will be gone one week. My driver and home are at your disposal as are my accounts in town if you need anything. I truly want to take care of you."

Luis gets up and straightens up his clothes as Anna shakes her head as if to say "no."

"Anna you have no choice. I hope by the time I return you will come to your senses and realize that I am the best thing that could happen to your drab life. Dump that old guy, turn your business over to us and think about our future together…traveling, dancing under the stars, making love day and night…think."

"I am sure that when I return," Luis continues, "Your decision will be the correct one."

Anna ponders Luis' last comment. Her mind is still racing, "Where is he going? I don't dare ask."

Luis holds her hand and then lifts it to his face and gently kisses it.

"One long week my love until I can see you and touch you again."

With that statement, he lets go of her hand, gives her a wink, picks up his coat and hat and leaves as quietly as he came. Rosa follows Luis to the door wagging her tail.

Anna waits a few minutes and then looks out of the window. Luis is walking down her walk to his car. It's as if his driver came out of nowhere to pick him up. Anna thinks, "It's just like Luis. He thinks he has the whole area on one large remote control."

The driver stops, gets out and opens the car door for Luis, then drives off.

Anna cannot stop staring out the window. She desperately wants to understand what just happened but can't. She believes everything happens for a reason and she will learn what the reason is.

Rosa comes back into the room; her head just seems to find its way under Anna's hand. She strokes it gently, "Rosa, I wonder what will happen to us? I know that he's evil but there is something wonderful about him. Something that makes me want to know more about him, the man, not the thug."

She starts to daydream about them romantically waking with a chill at the thought of such a thing happening in real life. Sometimes, however, life is filled with strange twists.

Anna sighs staring at the sky filled with pink tints and marshmallow clouds as it floats over the same green sea that leads to Jocko.

CHAPTER FIFTEEN
HUMBERTO

Luis' mentor and role model has always been his father, the late Humberto de la Monte. Luis could never live up to Humberto's dirty standards. By comparison, Luis is a philanthropist.

By the time he turned ten, Luis learned that he was the chosen one to keep the family drug running business alive. He watched as his Dad threatened local fishermen until he had their main fleet of boats under his thumb. With their unwilling assistance, Humberto would run drugs to his other dealers in Mexico and Florida. Captain Jocko was always a thorn in his side because he refused to cooperate with any of Humberto's demands.

A sea captain of old fashioned honor, Jocko hated anything that smelled of dishonesty. "The smell of lies," he often said, "is far worse than that of any rotten fish. I often wished that I could send my men in under cover of darkness and throw all of his damned cargo overboard, but I never wanted to put my crew in harm's way."

If Jocko were to give that command, his men would have gleefully obliged, throwing Humberto's precious bags of cocaine into the Gulf of Mexico. One night, after spending too much time personally emptying bottles of scotch, Jocko broke his promise to himself and really did issue the command. His men, drunk out of their minds, staggered onto Humberto's boat rousing up the other crew before the dawn's light. Nothing, however, was touched. Nothing was thrown overboard. Instead, the two inebriated crews offered to exchange rum bottles, angering both captains beyond words that these seafaring enemies could get along. At that point, Jocko commanded his crew to leave quickly, before Humberto's anger turned to violence.

The Captain from Seabliss would never take any unnecessary chances with his crew's safety even though he knew that he had something of great value, something Humberto wanted desperately. Jocko could never be totally sure of his own safety as well as that of his crew's. He breathed a deep sigh of relief that night when all made it back on his boat in one piece.

Humberto did not take Jocko's actions sitting down; he threatened Jocko's life many times in front of his crew. Jocko knew, however, that he could only taunt Humberto so far. Humberto had put the word out to the other captains not to harm Jocko until he found out where Jocko hid the goods. The senior drug dealer was privy to information that Jocko might be sitting on buried treasure thought to be a fortune in jewels. Humberto salivated at the thought of getting his hands on the treasure.

Humberto paid people to follow the captain's every move when in port hoping that he would lead them to the jewels' hiding place. Jocko was too smart for them; they learned nothing.

Humberto might have been brilliant in dealing cocaine, but was very lax about his own security. He thought it a smart move to keep Jocko out of harm's way until the old captain led him to the jewels. In reality, this decision may have led Humberto to his own demise. One day after his last public threat to Jocko, poor Humberto met his maker by mysteriously falling off a cliff overlooking his tiny Mexican homeport. Even though his fall was put on the record as an unfortunate accident, it has always served as the centerpiece for many different murder theories. No one has ever claimed to be a witness to what happened nor has anyone ever bragged of pushing the old pirate off the cliff. Luis, however, harbors his own theory one with Jocko as the prime suspect. Jocko has neither denied nor taken credit for any involvement.

A thorn in Luis' side, just the mere thought of Jocko makes Luis sees red; the same shade of red that a bull sees entering the ring. "I want Jocko gone once and for all. Out of my life. Not just because of my father, but because I want Anna and need her factory. With the old guy out of the way, I will have both."

Jocko permeates Luis' thoughts daily. He believes that Jocko was the last person to see his father alive and often wonders what really happed that day. Luis hopes that by "talking" to Jocko, he will get everything taken care of in one shot with the added benefit being that Luis will finally get the chance to avenge his father's death.

"Yes, Jocko my old friend. You will either have to cooperate or meet the fate my father's killer deserves. You will back off, give me the keys to the factory and let Anna come to my side."

With those thoughts, Luis prepares to leave Ojuana for the Florida Gulf Coast. He tells the local fisherman that he won't be smuggling cocaine into Florida on this run. Even as these lies exit his lips, Luis cannot resist any opportunity to make some extra money and fool the authorities.

He knows that the smaller boats as well as the smaller ports provide easier access. Ojuana exports many things, pottery, clay and marble statues and containers, onyx and stone to sell in Florida. Most of the fishing captains bring over some cargo for extra money. Luis chooses to send three marble benches having seats filled with bags of his white gold and then stuffed with newspapers on top. He also ships two clay pots and two small carved boxes empty for the purpose of fooling the authorities. This will be his last use of decoys until he gets his hands on Anna and Jocko's factory of course.

The guards and local authorities in Ojuana cooperate and look the other way for a few hundred American dollars each, small change compared to the street value of the merchandise.

"I enjoy sailing into the smaller barrier islands. The Coast Guard comes aboard to check for illegal aliens and merchandise but they don't have any of those well-trained drug-sniffing dogs like the larger ports. Without the dogs, my product is home free."

Luis prepares legitimate purchase orders for merchants in Florida before his departure. Most of the stores, landscapers, and garden centers have no idea that they are dealing with a drug lord. They just want the merchandise. He treats all of his customers very well and of course his prices are very hard to beat.

Besides giving killer deals, Luis is known to be generous. The Coast Guard appreciates his cooperation in their searches. He tells them how much he likes their work by leaving a few bottles of expensive tequila for their next party. This drug lord is a true chameleon able to fool anyone. He believes "There can never be too much goodwill especially in my line of work."

When his business is done, he rents a car and drives to Miami where he hires a private jet to fly the money along with himself to the Cayman Islands and his favorite private bank, The Grand Cayman Trust. He spends a few days there, enjoying the white beaches, snorkeling in the clear waters, and eating in the most expensive restaurants. His good looks usually allow him to meet some well to do and adventurous women looking for some forbidden love on vacation. He has spent many romantic nights on the beach making love under the stars to beautiful but married women pining for the attention they lack at home. This particular trip, however, is different. He will still enjoy the solitude of the underwater reefs, the restaurants and the rest, but Luis now has only one woman on his mind.

The Caymans is noted for another popular activity: jewelry shopping. Luis visits many of the gold merchants near the main port until he finds the most beautiful and large diamond engagement ring for Anna. He so wants to surprise her, to sweep her off of her feet. He wants nothing to do with any other women this trip. He manages to find an engagement ring with an enormous pink diamond set in platinum. Luis then makes sure that he leaves out enough cash for working capital after depositing a large sum in his Cayman Islands account.

Luis did not have enough time to find Jocko this trip but knows that he will go back to Florida soon. For now, however, he is content in the hopes that Anna will be pleasantly surprised to receive this beautiful ring.

She remains totally unaware of any of Luis' plans. Of course, Jocko is as well. Luis' ability to surprise his victim is one of his strong suits as past adversaries have realized.

"My next trip will be soon, short and successful. It'll be my big chance to make plans that work for our future. I should be in Seabliss no longer than a week. That should also give me enough time to get my containers unloaded, get through all of the port paperwork and customer schmoozing. If I play my cards right, my visit with Jocko shouldn't make my next trip any longer than a regular run."

Luis smiles at the thought of finally coming face to face with the old captain.

.

.

CHAPTER SIXTEEN
LUIS' GAME PLAN

A few weeks go by before Luis is preparing to venture off to Southwest Florida again. A great deal has happened in those three weeks. His love for Anna has grown stronger every day, but she refuses to let him into her heart. He surprised her with the ring. She will not wear it; Luis made her keep it. He believes that the day will come soon.

"This will really be my last business trip until I can fix things with Anna. I can't help it. Money to me is like chocolate to a chocoholic. The more I have; the more I need."

Of course the thought of outsmarting the authorities on either coast plays right into his extra large ego. The exchange rate of the dollar to the peso sweetens the pot even more.

"I'll be transporting another load of large containers filled with two sizes of Greek statues made to image those at my pool. Those rich Americans love to show them off in their gardens. I know that the bigger the container, the more hassle I will have with customs, but I'm not worried. I will play the old shell game with them making two different loads appear as one. The boats with the big statues will hide in the mangroves while my shells, their smaller versions, will remain empty and enter through proper channels. I will wine and dine local officials and remember the dockworkers with gifts."

Luis does not forget local customs official, Benjamin Crass. He looks at a small black velvet bag with a carat emerald in it for Crass' wife. When Crass gets this gift, Luis knows how easy it will be to pass through customs. "After all, there never can be too much good will. I will lay low and try to remain unnoticed. If Jocko gets the slightest inkling that I'm on my way to Seabliss, he will leave town as quickly as I arrive. Besides, if any of my customers realize how many millions I make with their "assistance," they would probably gag."

Luis prepares to board one of the small ships. "This trip will be very different. While I'm gone, I hope that magnificent ring as well as my love will bring Anna to her senses. She will convince Jocko to sign over his shares to me. I would hate to have to kill Jocko or even my Anna for the factory. I do love her but no-one can stand in my way."

The Southwest Florida coast boasts much of its mystique for drug runners because of its dense mangroves. Long ago, it was the favorite hiding place for pirates eager to shelter their own illegal cargo.

Mangroves have always been a smuggler's best friend. The area along the Florida coastline where Luis' main cargo boats intend to land is too rural to have any real entry ports, customs offices or drug-sniffing dogs. Boats entering through these waters are usually stopped by the Coast Guard using smaller ships. Their officers board the incoming vessels at sea to search for any illegal contents or passengers. Many small boats entering US waters this way are able to escape being searched because there are too few Coast Guard ships in the area. Without the dogs, officials have little reason to break open large containers. They have even less reason since Luis or his men can produce legitimate purchase orders for their contents. The nurseries and landscapers in the larger South Florida cities have no idea what Luis' true profession is; they only know how popular his clay products are and how much profit they can make from them.

This trip, the customs' clearance turns out to be much more complicated for the smaller containers than anticipated. Luis does not anchor his boat in one of the hidden landing sites but goes into one of the regular ports with all of the protocol. His small but empty containers are held up at the dock for days before getting cleared. There are new customs personnel on duty who take longer with the paperwork. It's just as well as Luis wants to throw them off the scent of his real load.

Upon arrival in one of the many mangrove inlets, the other boats with the containers containing life-sized statues are unloaded and prepared for the delivery trucks. Luis has canvassed this area for inlets where the trucks could easily set up portable loading docks. The boat captains signal their arrival with a high-pitched whistle only audible to dogs. The lead truck has two Dobermans who transmit the captain's command by barking. Not too far from shore, the driver lets the dogs go leading them to the right area.

The trucks then arrive rather quickly after that as they are waiting in a central location close by. They all have signs that read "Aztec Landscapers."

A closer inspection reveals that they have temporary adhesive signs covering the real signs for "Tropical Truck Rentals." Looking at the line up from the loading dock, at least a half a dozen other trucks with bogus signs are awaiting Luis' cargo for processing and repacking.

Once his men empty the statues and unpack the bags of cocaine, they place them in small airtight metal boxes. It feels like forever, but finally Luis' men gets the OK to pick up the containers filled with decoys and take them to his warehouse about eight miles from the docks where they can be properly prepped with the other containers.

Luis will soon be able to begin his meetings with the local drug dealers in towns and cities that dot this coastal region. The dealers will be even hungrier than normal for the cocaine due to a recent interception of another shipment from another dealer.

Obviously, Luis' deal with the statues goes extremely well. The local drug dealers sweeten the pot and pay handily for the remaining white gold. They too pick up their expensive cargo using fake landscaping trucks at Luis' hidden warehouse.

Luis is paid well and in cash; his statues pay for all of his shipping costs.

This area has a long history of drug runners coming in and out of the mangroves without ever being caught. Luis hopes that this coastal region will take decades to develop; hopefully long enough for him to retire on his private yacht and set sail for the Mediterranean. Luis does not worry so much about change in the small Mexican ports. He knows that he will remain the king there with or without Jocko for a long, long time.

Now that his work is over, Luis is ready to find Jocko and take care of his most important business. Who knows? With all his cash, Luis may just buy the factory from Jocko offering a price that the old man could not resist.

"I need to have a talk with that old man. He needs to make Anna come around to my way of thinking. Of course, she may resent me for the rest of my life, but that's the chance I must take. Jocko has to tell Anna that he no longer needs her. He must break her heart. I'll destroy him if he doesn't. I hope that this time will be the charm because without her factory, I am running out of legal options to use for shipping. No more drugs, no more cash, perish the thought, no more lifestyle."

As deep as Luis' distrust is for Jocko, he remains a gentleman who would like to have a "discussion" with the Captain first. "If I can get into his home,

I just might be able to quietly talk some sense into Jocko. I can't tell Anna about my plans or she will warn him."

No, Luis can and will only trust one contact in Florida. She too has an axe to grind with the old sea captain. It is Jocko's ex-wife, Bella. It can be a very small world sometimes, one that makes strange bedfellows. Luis knows that infidelity is something a woman does not forget and rarely forgives. Bella, who has been down that road, now stays as far away from Jocko as she can even though as a manager's wife, she does have access to his apartment.

Luis thinks, "I'll call Bella. I will tell her I need to talk to Jocko alone. She'll be all too happy to let me into his condo where I can surprise him." Luis smiles. "Bella would stop at nothing to make Jocko's life miserable. Her new husband knows that as well and tries his best to keep his wife and Jocko apart."

Luis goes through his address book. "Ah Bella, beautiful Bella. Here's her number, Bella Taggert. I will call her now and ask for her help." Luis is careful to find an out of the way phone booth, deposits his money and dials her number. "If her husband answers, I'll hang up and try again. She'll know that that's my signal."

Luis hears the phone ring. A woman's voice answers, "Hello." Luis smiles so widely that his gold crown glistens in the sunlight.

"Bella, my beautiful Bella, It is your Luis. You cannot imagine how wonderful it is to hear your voice."

"And yours my son. Where are you now? Tell me so that I can give you directions to the condo. Are you ready?"

"More than you can ever imagine." Luis answers quickly. He knows that this will be the right time as Bella gives him the directions.

CHAPTER SEVENTEEN
BELLA TAGGERT

After Luis' call, Bella Taggert sits comfortably on her lanai watching a patch of clouds float over the back bay. Their movements mesmerize her, making her mind wander back to her younger days in Mexico. The pastel sky tones remind her of the sky she saw from the small window of her parents' cement cottage in her hometown.

"That sky is just as beautiful as the sky was on the day that Jocko and I married. We were so young then and so in love. In some ways, it feels like a century has passed since our wedding and yet in others, it's just like yesterday."

Just the mere thought of Jocko's name provokes a deep and unforgiving anger in Bella. "Jocko, hah, he convinced me to leave my beloved hometown to move here to Florida. He said that our love would last forever."

"He never realized how lonely I was here. He would go for months at a time and I hardly knew anyone in town. The people I met here didn't speak my language. I gave that selfish man everything I had, my love, my care and my loyalty and how does he repay me? He repays me by dumping me for that younger woman. I hate the both of them with a passion. I'm so glad when the old goat is dead. I can't wait to spit on his grave."

There has never been anyone or anything that could ease Bella's pain or arrest her anger. "I remember how numb and out of touch I felt the day that Jocko told me that he was leaving and wanted a divorce. I know I'm lucky to be married, but Skip is not the same."

She found it more than odd that her new husband would accept the position of condo manager in the same building where Jocko lives. All the years since they separated, she has tried to avoid Jocko. She refuses to go into his apartment no matter what is wrong. No matter how hard she tries, she still runs into him. It still hurts her to look at him. The pain doubles whenever Anna comes to visit. "When I see those two traitors together, I wish I had a big knife so that I could stab them together."

Bella knows that Skip Taggert is a good steady man. She also knows that he provides well for her and loves her, but something is still missing in their relationship. The thrill of Jocko's touch and the excitement in his romance cannot be duplicated.

"Why is the first love so hard to forget?" she often asks herself. Jocko was Bella's and even though he left her flat, she still would take him back in a heartbeat. "After Jocko moved out, I had to work as a maid in another small rental complex in order to make enough money to live. That's where I met Skip."

Skip worked as the maintenance man in that same building. Taggert may not be the brightest bulb in the chandelier but he isn't the dimmest either. Bella and Taggert are the same age. He is a little shorter than she is but looks much older from his days at sea. Bella married him because she thought at her age she was lucky to have any suitor let alone a steady hard-working guy like him.

Bella confesses silently, "I know Skip hates Jocko as much as I do; at times maybe even more. I think their mutual disrespect goes back to their days at sea, but I'm not sure."

She isn't sure because Taggert has never discussed it with her. Maybe his reason stems from their time at sea but it also may be quite different than she thinks. Taggert hates to witness the look of longing in Bella's eyes whenever she sees Jocko outside and the deep look of hurt when Bella watches Anna and Jocko walking together. Taggert wonders after each of these brief encounters if Bella dreams of Jocko when they make love, a thought he loathes and one that drives him crazy.

Bella doesn't realize that if Taggert could have his way with Jocko, he would happily push the old guy off his lanai or do whatever it takes to get the old goat out of their lives for good.

Bella does know that Luis has an even bigger axe to grind with Jocko than she does. She looks forward to his arrival and plans to keep it a big secret.

CHAPTER EIGHTEEN
SEABLISS TODAY

In the hours since Jocko's death, the afternoon sky absorbs the island's sorrow and returns all the tears in the form of a light misty rain. Bill is at the county medical examiner's office waiting for Doc to advise him as to Jocko's cause of death as well as go over any conclusions thus far.

Doc finally ambles into the county morgue obviously in no hurry to open the stainless steel drawer holding Jocko's remains again. Opening that drawer just re-opens the bad memories of the autopsy for him, but Doc realizes that Bill needs to know how to proceed with the case. Doc wants Jocko's death treated with respect no matter how hard the process is for him. He stiffly slides the cold drawer open and partially removes the sheet covering the Captain.

"Did you notice the lines around his mouth?" Bill asks as Doc looks over the body again. Bill is so busy looking for additional clues on the body that he does not notice Doc's hands shaking. Just looking at Jocko all sewn up reminds the good doctor of what he had to do.

Bill continues, 'You know I never really noticed them at the apartment. Did you? Mariah mentioned something."

Doc does not respond. He pulls out his tape recorder to listen to his recording, "Captain Jocko Compton, age 77, died of an apparent heart attack. Autopsy in progress because no attending physician present at the time of death."

"Judging by the levidity of the body, Jocko died right in that chair just the way he was found. Rigor mortis has already begun to set in. His eyes were wide open and his jaw dropped. My guess is that our patient has been dead about 26-28 hours making the time of death between ten A.M. and twelve noon on August 9, 1986 Body temperature in the lab confirms this. There are signs of vomiting and uncontrollable diarrhea. His left arm shows signs of bruising and multiple needle marks. Looking at the physical condition of the body, there are thin red lines around sides of mouth. Multiple needle marks in his left arm which appear larger than they normally might be."

"There is mild bruising around the needle marks. Patient was a diabetic on insulin. I will now proceed with the blood work."

"I am about to cut into Captain's chest."

"All aspect's of the heart's condition suggests that the patient died from sudden congestive heart failure. There is evidence of tachycardia putting stress on the heart and causing an atrioventricular blockage. As his primary physician, I have to admit I saw no symptoms of this in any exam or tests prior to his demise. I just gave him his yearly physical about a month ago and Jocko's heart tested to be in good shape. I find this to be more than a bit odd though it may not be totally unusual. I'd like to note again that the patient was a diabetic. I will now examine the stomach and kidneys."

Doc shuts the tape recorder off and looks at Bill, "I don't envy your job. Did you find any next of kin?"

Bill shrugs his shoulders, "None in Florida Doc. Well, really no legal ones that I could find in the U.S. I got Johnson checking on Mexico. The old guy spent a lot of time there. The records over there are pretty primitive. The church keeps them all and some are by word of mouth only so Johnson has his job cut out for him."

Doc gives Bill a reassuring look, "Hey, man, that's all you can do. You're doing your best."

Bill smiles, "Thanks Doc, I appreciate that. I guess I'll wait for your interpretation of the lab results back at the station."

Meanwhile on the other side of the island, Mariah is still grieving knowing full well that she must return to her store to make sure that everything is all right in case she'll have to leave again. It's odd how something so routine as being in the store can be consoling.

Of course, word of Jocko's death spread quickly. Customers, islanders, even some of the tourists are coming into the store repeating the horrible news of the day's events adding embellishments to each retelling. Mariah soon tires of hearing, "Sorry to hear about the old Captain, Mariah. Do you know what really happened? We've heard all kinds of terrible things." She refuses to respond to many of the questions especially those from the dentist's wife, Mrs. Langley, notorious for altering facts and spreading fiction as if it were fact.

Mariah feels no need to contribute any more to the old woman's treasure trove of lies and politely walks away. She is still very concerned, however, because she has not heard a word from Bill and desperately wants to know the real cause of Jocko's death.

Meanwhile, Bill is back at the office typing his preliminary report. Doc, still at the morgue, gulps a few swigs from his flask calming his frazzled nerves as he reads the test results. Mariah retreats to her office at the store. Looking in the mirror, she can see that her eyes are still red and puffy. Poor Spike can't calm her down by putting his big furry head under her hand. She knows that she should be strong and return to work. She just won't discuss anything about Jocko.

The only new news is gossip and that kind of news spreads as quickly as kudzu. She and Spike sit in the small almost closet sized office for at least fifteen minutes before she regains her composure enough to talk to customers again.

Mariah takes another tissue from her purse and dries her eyes. She looks over at her faithful pet. "I just can't believe that we lost him. He's our very best friend. We have to get to the bottom of this; I know that something isn't right."

"O.K, I'm ready. Let's go to work "she sighs. She opens the office door as Spike pushes his way out ahead of her. They go behind the counter only to be greeted with more questions. Mariah remains quiet appearing to still be in shock. Shane had already heard the awful news, long before she could tell him

"Mariah, I am so sorry to hear about Jocko." Shane is trying to console her. In a funny way, he does. Mariah knows that if anything, Shane is honest. "I'm sorry that you have to listen to so much scuttlebutt. Some townsfolk need a life. Who let the information go public anyway?" Mariah does not respond. Shane lets up on all of the questions. She turns her back to him as if preparing to check the daily work totals since she has been gone. It's only been a little over five hours but there are phone messages and problems with orders that need her attention. When she catches up, she wonders about the autopsy results.

"I haven't heard from Bill. Maybe I should call him." Mariah thinks as she looks over at the T.V. and notices it blank with a blue screen. She finds a tape on the counter and puts it in the VCR. Ironically, it is another copy of 'Appointment With Death', the same movie Jocko had been watching.

Mariah's head hurts as much as her heart. She blocks out the noise from the movie as well as the dull sounds of customer conversations about Jocko.

She remembers Jocko sitting up in the chair expressionless, his apartment in total disarray. His house is always spotless so this mess is highly unusual and very suspicious.

"Not like my house" she thinks, "My house hasn't been neat since the bank appraiser came by for the mortgage rewrite." Her sense of observation is very keen. It has to be to run a retail store. She is used to taking a visual inventory just by walking past the shelves. She can tell if something is off with just a quick perusal.

In that same manner, her mind mentally circles Jocko's living room as if on an inventory search. Her thoughts stop abruptly. "The sliders were open…the cigarette butt on the floor… Could it have been Pacco's? It was a Mexican cigarette. What about those two holes in Jocko's arm? Why two holes? He never missed. That doesn't make any sense either. I'm right. I know that I'm right. He was murdered…"

She mentally goes over the facts again "Did Jocko inject himself twice on purpose or was someone else there? The whole thing makes no sense to me."

Just as she is rehashing the crime scene in her mind, a master sleuth named Poirot is also asking questions of his suspects on the screen behind her.

Mariah turns and looks up at the small TV thinking," I would've made a great detective. I ask questions and never accept things at face value. I love that guy."

With all of the clutter going through her mind right now, she misses most of the movie's dialogue but does hear the master sleuth say one word, "poison." "Poison, "Mariah repeats," I wonder if Jocko could have been the victim of a lethal dose of a drug as well. But why? And who would do such a thing?"

She doesn't realize that she is speaking out loud. "So it was murder," she whispers.

"Murder? Did you say murder?" Shane repeats.

Mariah is surprised; she must have been thinking out loud.

"Oh no Shane, I'm talking about the movie."

Mariah then puts her head in her hands and leans down on the counter; she hopes this will make her brain work harder. She closes her eyes hoping for a transformational thought.

Her thoughts, however, are soon interrupted again as hears one word in the dialogue. That one word is a potent one. Moonbeam has often explained to her that the cosmos has winds that two spiritually connected people can hear at the same time. Maybe that's the case here; maybe it's just a coincidence but at the same moment that Mariah hears that word, Bill who returned from the morgue and is sitting at his small desk in the cramped police department, hears that same word after he picks up his phone.

It's Doc on the other end. Bill is curious, "Hey man what's going on? Any news on Jocko?"

Doc's voice sounds very serious, "I have one word for you my friend, and that's digitoxin. We still have to find out how much he ingested. I'll call when I have more news."

Mariah is half listening to the movie when one word from its dialogue stands out to her. "Digitoxia. Digitoxia?" Mariah thinks as she repeats the word. "Digitoxia." I wonder if that's the same as "Digitoxin." She listens intently to the explanation of how it works; it is a fast acting poison that in lethal doses gives its victim the symptom of a heart attack.

"I have to get this info to Bill. Maybe Doc could check for this out for us," Mariah thinks.

The thought of someone planning to harm her Jocko makes her despondent again. "Why would anyone want to do in a sweet man like Jocko?"

She looks around for Shane. "Shane…Shane…"

He is putting away movies in the back, "I can hear you Mariah."

"Shane I'm going for about a half hour. Mike should be here any minute. It's almost six. Tell him I'll see him later or at closing."

Mariah checks the register to make sure that the store has enough change and makes sure that Shane has returned all of the videos on his shift so that they could be rented out again. She then looks down at Spike who is on his side sleeping behind the counter. She gently rubs his head. "Hey boy, Let's go for a ride"

Spike's ears almost stand up straight. He jumps up and starts kissing her. Mariah grabs her keys, opens the glass front door to the store. Spike jumps into the car and sits up straight on the fake black and white cow skin seat covers.

"Oh no our seats are wet. It must have rained. I'm so stressed that I left the top down. My mind is full of other things right now, Spike. Get out and stay here, I'll get some beach towels out of the trunk."

Spike waits as if at attention and watches Mariah cover their seats with the towels. He climbs back onto the passenger seat as soon as she finishes.

She always says 'Start your engines'. Spike relishes those words lifting his nose in the air in anticipation of feeling those refreshing Gulf breezes. Mariah picks up speed and Spike lets out a loud howl of delight. Mariah hates when he does this because she can never sneak up on anyone. Besides, tourists think Spike strange. At any rate, off they go Spike's bandana flapping in the wind and Mariah's long hair blowing as well.

Her red convertible makes a bold U-turn and heads straight for the police station. By now, Bill is sitting at his desk, light on, feet up, staring at a box of things from Jocko's apartment. He puts on a pair of latex gloves and aimlessly rifles through Jocko's personal effects scrutinizing every single item hoping that one will tell him a story. Bill looks puzzled not by what's there but by what is missing. The night air is cool so he left the front door open using the screen slider. After all, this is Florida and there are plenty of noseeums.

Bill's office is around the corner from the main commercial district of the island. Mariah finds a space right in front. She parks the car and Spike barks as if to alert Bill as he tries to jump over her in an effort to get out first.

"Sure hope Bill found out something." Mariah thinks. Mariah knows that Bill's still there because she sees the light on.

Bill hears the ruckus and knows that they're coming. He opens the drawer with the dog treats in anticipation. When Mariah and Spike enter, it's like a tornado strikes the room. First the champion dog treat eater of all time, and then Miss Curiosity. Bill smiles as they enter, "Why me? Why do I have to be tortured? Here I am trying to deal seriously with a real case."

Mariah doesn't find his remarks funny. She's hoping to finally get some serious answers. "Hey Bill, did you find out anything? Is the autopsy finished? How about the tests? Did you stay through the whole thing?"

Bill shakes his head, "Hey Mariah slow it up. Ask me one question at a time. Doc just called with the lab results. Seems your movie-watching hunch may be right. Jocko had high levels of digitoxin in his system. That would explain why we thought it was a heart attack. I am trying to sort…"

"Did you say digitoxin? Case? "Mariah interrupts. "So it was murder, Digitoxia like the movie." Mariah continues, "I have been wracking my brain all day trying to think who would even think of doing such a horrible thing to Jocko. I am blank, totally blank. Although I must say I have met some unusual people since yesterday."

Bill looks up "Strange people huh? They must be really strange if you put them in that category with all the characters in your store. Why didn't you tell me about this before?"

Mariah smiles, "You would've said that I spend too much time with Moonbeam. Now I guess they are important. So tell me what Doc said exactly..."

Bill cracks a smile, "Well, first of all, he definitely wanted me to convey to you how much he hates doing autopsies...hates... he wanted me to repeat that..."

Mariah looks up at Bill wryly, "That's my Doc, hold their hand and give them a Kleenex, but no blood please. Did Doc say that my power of deduction is incredible or brilliant? Exactly which of those two words did he chose?'

"Neither my dear, neither" Bill responds quickly. "Doc isn't positive that someone else gave Jocko the overdose. Maybe that city doctor gave Jocko a prescription for his heart that we didn't know about. Doc is calling him to find out to make sure that Jocko didn't just give himself an accidental overdose. You know how older people can get depressed and we don't even recognize the symptoms."

Mariah's face becomes so red at that thought that if she were a volcano, hot lava would come out of her mouth. "Bill, don't insult my intelligence. Don't insult poor Jocko. He would not and I repeat not commit suicide either accidentally or on purpose!"

Her arms are folded as she marches over to the desk. "William if you know anything you better damn well tell me. Jocko was like a father to me. Understand?"

Bill is somewhat surprised by her last remark. He wants to change the subject. "How did you two manage to get out of the store? Didn't the boy moan and groan?"

"Well I'm the boss," Mariah interjects, "and I just left. Shane knows how badly I want to find out about Jocko."

The phone rings again. Bill jumps from his chair and answers. He looks at Mariah, puts his hand over her mouth to hush her up and says, "Hey Doc."

Mariah's heart begins to pound. She listens intently to Bill's side of the conversation. Bill looks distressed, "Yeah, so it was definite. No prior prescription. Uh huh, Well, I guess we have to upgrade this case to a homicide and proceed with a murder investigation."

Mariah hears this and starts pacing around the very compact office. She is pensive yet anxious to speak at the same time. "I knew it," she says talking to herself out loud, "Suicide is not for Jocko and he was in perfect health. Imagine them thinking suicide…ridiculous, absolutely ridiculous. It's amazing that they didn't listen to me. We have lost hours of valuable time. The killers could be in South America by now or just hiding on a boat in the mangroves ready to go out into the Gulf leaving no trace of ever having being here. Well Sherlock where do we go from here?" Mariah's arms are folded around her mid-section like an Indian snake charmer.

Bill pays no attention to Mariah's longwinded conversation. He wants to hear all that Doc has to say. Bill asks calmly, "How was it administered? Really…huh… How much? It had to be someone he knew. How else could they get that close to him? "Mariah cannot stand the suspense any longer. She blurts out, "Bill, tell me right now what Doc is saying. What really happened to Jocko? There are two people in this room, you know. Was I right? Tell me Bill…Talk to me…" Mariah starts to cry out of shear frustration

Bill is winding down the conversation. "Thanks Doc, we'll be in touch." Bill puts the receiver down and looks at Mariah with that kind facial expression that usually precedes bad news. "OK Mariah…Calm down. There's nothing more we can do for Jocko other than rationally try to find out who did this. Before I tell you I need you to raise your right hand."

Mariah looks puzzled. "I'm making you a deputy for this case only. You understand that all information is confidential and that you will respond for work on this case when needed and I should have asked."

Mariah smiles, "I do."

"OK then. Doc says that the lab found high levels of digitoxin in the old guy's blood. The levels were high enough to create the symptoms of a massive heart attack to the untrained eye. Let me finish." Bill could sense that Mariah is about to interrupt. "Digitoxin according to Doc is a drug used to treat heart problems like congestive heart failure if used correctly. It can be absorbed orally or injected into a muscle or administered through an IV. If too much is administered, the victim's pulse slows way down, interfering with the heart's contractions. The blood flowing to the heart increases and causes the victim to have a heart attack. The drug reaction time if given the proper dosage is immediate. My paramedics were right in their diagnosis. They just didn't realize that Jocko's heart attack was forced. "So," Bill goes on, "To the untrained eye, Jocko's cause of death would have been written up as a heart attack."

Mariah is quiet. All those critics who say she watches too many movies better be quiet now. Every now and then, she does pick up some new information. "Was I the only one to see Jocko's veins, that all of his small veins had ruptured. That was about the only trace evidence the killer had to worry about. If I hadn't seen that, he or she would have had the perfect crime."

Bill smiles, "Yes, you were right. Those veins were the only clues; he or she might have gotten away Scot free except for you. Jocko would be proud of you... Very proud."

Bill wipes away tears from Mariah's eyes. She is quiet, highly unusual for her. She finally looks up at him as he continues. "Here's what we know... The medicine overdose was administered through a needle with his normal insulin injection. That means someone he knew and trusted either prepared the mixture for him and or injected him."

"Or," Mariah continues, "Someone may have switched the bottles and Jocko injected himself unaware that the bottle had been tampered with." Bill sighs deeply," That's my girl... Now you're thinking. His apartment is still sealed so we can go back and try to relive his last hours."

Bill realizes that he has to assuage her feelings "Mariah" Bill starts, "I have to hand it to you girl. We never would have investigated Jocko's death like this. After all, how many 'white collar' homicides do we have in Seabliss? If a murder happens during a bar fight, there's always a knife or injury that focuses on the crime. It's pretty cut and dry."

Mariah by now is beaming with pride in the knowledge that she was right all along.

Bill continues, "The apartment is still sealed. We should go take another look."

"Sealed?" Mariah repeats loudly and slowly, "Sealed my foot. Since you left, a couple of unusual people have been in and out of there. How on earth can you possibly consider a crime scene 'sealed' with no locks or anyone guarding the door You know Skip could care less. He got his real estate license last year. The quicker we are all out of there the quicker he can sell the apartment for Jocko's heirs and make himself a big commission."

"At one point I thought I was standing as you say in Grand Central Station."

Bill looks surprised, "Well is that so Miss Know-It-All. Why were you there so long anyway? Let's take a ride over there right now so that I can see what's what."

Obviously he is game but Mariah is a little slower to respond, pulling her hair back and banding it a sign that she is ready for business. "OK Bill Let's really go check it out now that we know I was right. Don't forget to bring rubber gloves and any testing kits we might need." Bill looks annoyed. He hates anyone telling him how to do his job, especially a back seat driver.

"Come on Spike." The three exit the station and head for Bill's jeep. Spike of course jumps in first heading for the back seat. Mariah and Bill take Spike back to the store. They then go on to Jocko's hoping to catch a killer.

CHAPTER NINETEEN

Armed with new information, Mariah and Bill are both anxious to start their re-examination of the facts. This time they arrive without all of the pomp and circumstance of police car sirens and flashing lights.

Bill parks his jeep; they unobtrusively go up the stairs to the Captain's. They do not want to rouse old Taggert. They open the front door as quietly as possible. As they enter the small apartment, Bill breathes a sigh of relief that the crime scene tape is still in tact. Looking through the doorway, he can see that the place looks pretty much like it did the last time he saw it; but his eyes are not as focused as Mariah's.

Mariah's eyes move as quickly as a searchlight taking a quick inventory as she looks through the front doorway and over the yellow crime tape. Her mind wanders back to her brief encounters with Pacco and Anna. "I'm still baffled by how quickly they appeared after Jocko's death."

Bill pulls off some of the yellow crime scene tape making a path for them to enter. Mariah's eyes are still rotating around the room. "What are we looking for exactly?" She asks Bill as she walks around the living room and then wanders into the small galley kitchen.

Bill is also engrossed in the moment responding with an "I don't really know. I guess anything out of the ordinary, anything no matter how insignificant. If you find something that meets that description you'll know immediately."

Mariah puts on a pair of rubber gloves and starts digging through the short mound of papers on the countertop. The messy mound alone is an unusual scene in this usually meticulous apartment. "I seem to remember leaving things the way I found them. Someone else must have been through them since I left," Mariah thinks.

She picks up each piece of paper carefully looking for a clue. No disposable needle wrappers, nothing strange. So she starts on the wastepaper basket "Aha look here Sherlock, another cigarette butt...Jocko didn't smoke cigarettes, he enjoyed his pipe." Mariah carefully picks the paper up with tweezers and places it in a bag.

"Great Mariah how many cigarette smokers did Jocko know especially from the docks? Let me take a look. Well, this one narrows our search to all cigarette smokers who roll their own."

Mariah still believes this to be an important find. "Well, I'm going to bag it anyway because it may be important and it's different than the other one. Jocko was so fastidious that he would never leave a butt in the trash because it would smell. He emptied his trash daily. When we consider that with the fact that this is the garbage from the day he died, that little butt may be of big significance."

Bill is very quiet. He always is when she might be right. Mariah feels like she is on a roll so she continues, "If we look at the brand mark, we can see that it's in Spanish or perhaps Mexican, a fact that may narrow down our search. We can rule out Taggert as well as you and me. In this case, I consider everyone else a suspect."

Bill looks up, "Not so fast Mariah, Taggart's wife is Mexican. I guess only you and I are the only ones off the hook. I'd just as soon leave him on as he showed no sincere sadness at Jocko's passing."

Mariah starts to walk away from Bill and walks over to Jocko's chair. She knows that the clues are there; she just doesn't see them. She walks around the chair slowly. Bill, already in the kitchen area, starts to speak to himself, "I know there has to be something here. We have to find anything odd, anything out of place, no matter how mundane this thing may appear. I'm sure with Mariah's eagle eyes she'll see it first!"

Mariah snaps her plastic gloves nervously like a kid snaps bubble gum. The plastic makes a loud noise. "Anything odd." Mariah laughs thinking, "If Bill came to search my house, everything would qualify."

She begins to look around methodically sifting through one item at a time. The books and magazines seem as tall as a mountain, a neat mountain but a mountain nevertheless. She notices something pushed in the middle.

She reaches in and finds a journal: Jocko's journal. She goes over to a small living room chair now covered in plastic and sits down hoping to read its entries for any clues, but all that is inside are nautical directions and accounts of sea voyages. She opens the journal skipping through the pages quickly. Before she can continue looking for clues, something else catches her eyes.

"Look at this." She continues to approach the item. "I remember how Jocko used to feed Spike treats from this." She continues to approach that one item slowly almost like a heron stalking its prey. The item that her eyes focus on is Jocko's cane.

She picks it up. The ornate top with large sterling silver dolphins falls off abruptly.

"Hey Bill, this is odd. Someone else has been here. They must have been looking for something in this cane. They must have believed Jocko's jokes about hiding a fortune somewhere. They must have wanted whatever was in there." Mariah, still wearing gloves, picks up the bottom of the cane. Unscrewing the middle, Mariah peers inside. 'Bill someone else has been here all right. Do you even hear what I'm saying?" Mariah kneels down and turns the cane upside down. She takes out a small screwdriver from her purse and twists open a funny looking large screw that appears to hold the cane together. The cane comes apart in two sections. One has a tiny lock that looks like a master lock with a numerical code. It must be the secret compartment.

"Wow, Jocko wasn't kidding. He had a secret compartment!"

"Nice try Mariah but how much a of a secret can it be if you can find it and yes I have heard every word. If that's the case, we should bring it in for prints." Mariah then turns the lock with the numbers. It opens without a code because someone else had already opened it. Mariah then shakes that part of the cane as hard as a bartender does a martini. It's empty except for some very tiny sand like granules. Bill watches intently, "OK Mariah It's empty so what?"

"What you don't understand is that Jocko claimed that he always hid things in that compartment, the one below where he kept a few treats for Spike. Jocko used to joke about his secret retirement fund. I always thought he was kidding but since it's open and empty maybe he was telling the truth." Mariah does not move. Bill puts his hands in the air as if stopping traffic. He instructs her "Stay right where you are. Don't move an inch."

Bill walks over and stands near Mariah careful not to step in the granules. He holds the cane up to the light and examines it carefully. He is mesmerized. "You mean that the old guy could have stashed a lot of cash in here?" Mariah ponders for a moment, "He could have but it's unlikely. I think it may be something smaller but worth big money. At any rate the cane's empty now."

Bill is still thinking about what might have been in there. His eyes then go back to the floor where Mariah shook the cane. He grabs a flashlight from his back pocket to take a closer look at the granules. They are shiny. He pulls his small magnifying glass out from his shirt pocket and looks at the shiny dust. "Look at this, the dust is green…tiny fragments of emerald green glass." Bill also wearing gloves reaches for his flat edge screwdriver and scrapes the glass fragments into a bag. "You know Mariah these could be emeralds. If that's the case, we now have motive for robbery along with homicide leading us to someone who knew him well."

He looks at Mariah. "Imagine that, old Jocko may have been walking around town with a cane filled with emeralds. I bet they were very valuable emeralds from his travels to South America. I'll have to run some tests to be sure, but my theory about robbery and homicide looks like a sure bet now. Jocko was probably murdered and robbed by someone who knew about his secret stash."

Mariah blurts in before Bill could get too carried away with himself. "You know Jocko walked everywhere with that cane. He came in the store and opened its top in front of people to give Spike a treat."

Bill answers slowly, "Yeah, but my guess is there was a barrier to the second part or our old Captain would have gotten knocked off years ago. Let's take this bag of dust to the lab to make sure that we are dealing with real emeralds." Just before they are about to leave, Mariah opens Jocko's bedroom door a crack.

"Bill wait," Mariah sounds surprised, "Look at his bedroom. All of the drawers are open and ransacked. Oh, my gosh, there are clothes and stuff all over the place. Someone wanted something pretty badly. Do you think that there is more to this than the emeralds?"

Bill walks into the bedroom ahead of her to check it out. His hand is on his gun. "Whoever it was, they're gone. I'm going to dust for prints and then we'll go to the lab."

Mariah follows Bill in. "Jocko had more in his life then we know about…" She pauses, "Maybe you're right, maybe I do watch too many movies but we should organize our facts."

Bill gets his kit out and proceeds to try and find some fingerprints on the drawers. Mariah looks deep in thought as she thinks about the sweet old man that was her friend and wonders how much more she would find out about him.

"Hey girl, don't look so sad. Are you ready to go to the lab? I'm going to need to fingerprint you to eliminate yours from the pack. Then we can start putting together a list of possible suspects and get their prints."

"'Suspects'. That's hard when they're all people we haven't met yet," Mariah interjects.

"Mariah, Let's bring in what we got to the lab and grab a cup of coffee and something to eat at Murdock's. I don't know about you but I haven't eaten all day. It'll help us think. You're right; we mentally need to reorganize the facts. That emerald dust if that's what it is didn't come from Oz and the thief didn't disappear in a tornado…so maybe with a little help from Donny in the lab we can find the Yellow Brick Road that will lead us straight to the wizard."

"Sounds like a good idea Bill," Mariah smiling at his movie references." But suppose our killer is someone we haven't met yet?"

"Mariah, we have to start processing clues somewhere and this is a logical start." Bill starts packing up his equipment.

"Bill, did you ever think that we might need a different kind of help…maybe even some special help….like the kind Moonbeam offers. May I take one of Jocko's possessions to her for advice?"

Bill looks up as if totally caught off guard. He responds, "I thought you said Moonbeam can be full of malarkey. Now you want a wanna be psychic to crack a case that any expert would find hard. Give me a break!"

He looks into Mariah's eyes. He sees that she is desperate because of her love for Jocko. Mariah knows how to lay on the charm. "OK, if it will make you feel better but nothing more significant than a pair of socks from the bedroom OK?"

Mariah smiles. She can sense that her negotiations are making progress as they have gone from from a "no" to "socks."

"Thanks Bill I appreciate that but socks is not exactly what I had in mind."

"Mariah Don't even think about taking that cane" Bill says quickly hoping to respond with a verbal preemptive strike.

Mariah looks disappointed, "But Bill, Moonbeam should have something intrinsic to the case to read. The cane is something that Jocko treasured. He always had it with him," she replies as she reaches for the unusual walking stick. "Besides, it may have been the last thing he touched. If the lab gets it first, Moonbeam's powers are diminished."

"Nice try Mariah but the cane should go for fingerprint testing and not alien diagnosing."

Bill bags the cane in clear plastic. Mariah never accepts Bill's decisions as final. She knows that he's a softie and she can break him. He loads the evidence in the back seat of his jeep so that he can keep it locked up in case they stop at Murdock's before the lab. This way they can keep an eye on the jeep from the front windows.

Bill picks up the remaining evidence bags; Mariah follows. They load the last of the plastic bags; both are unaware that all the while, they are all being watched.

CHAPTER TWENTY

Mariah hops in the jeep just as Bill starts to pull out of the parking lot. Their latest find may be just what's needed to crack the case. They each have a great deal to think about and are so deep in thought that they fail to notice a person standing in the shadows outside of Jocko's building watching them. The shadowy figure waits for them to leave, then gets into a small dark car and follows at a distance intending to keep a close eye on them both and the cane.

Bill and Mariah enter Murdock's Cafe looking a bit tired, but they realize they have to keep going. "Hey, Betty, we'll have a booth near the front window." The waitresses all know Bill and were told by the owners to take good care of him. "Sure, Bill, follow me. Our grouper special looks great today!"

Bill quickly orders, "Great, we'll take two with some coffee, please."

Betty then leads Mariah and Bill to a booth overlooking their locked police jeep. They are relieved that they made a quick stop at the lab to leave the green glassy dust and cigarette butts with the tech Donny. Mariah is very happy because she was able to talk Bill into holding onto the cane for a short while longer. The plastic wrapped cane is lying on the floor of the back seat. They need to sit near the window to keep an eye on it.

Murdock's Coffee Shop is one of the busiest places on the island. Partially because of its location, but mostly because of the fresh seafood, large portions and affordable prices, unlike the tourist traps that dot the main street. Murdock's is a favorite with the locals and it's not too far from Mariah's shop. Its cedar walls remind patrons of Old Florida. It has large windows with café style curtains that cover the top third of the window. The tables are dark blue Formica with matching chrome chairs that date back to the fifties. There are different colored booths lining the big front windows.

The Murdock family boasts proud fisherman and their walls show it. They proudly display photos of different generations with their catch of large sharks.

Smaller colorful catches that have been preserved also dot the walls.

Bill and Mariah try to get comfortable as they put on their thinking caps over a cup of coffee and wait for the special. As they talk and motion with their hands, that same pair of eyes that watched them at Jocko's is now in the hibiscus bushes across the street from Murdock's. As this mystery person watches them through the large window that faces the main street, a big smile comes over his or her face. It's a smile that denotes victory.

Mariah is squirming around in the burgundy vinyl booth. Bill has turned his paper placemat upside down, drawing a bunch of arrows with his pen as if planning a football play. "OK Mariah. We have the cigarette butt, the probable emerald dust and whatever info you dug up improperly reading Jocko's journal and mail. Don't look so glum I actually think that we're making progress."

Mariah is not so optimistic. "Bill I want to see Moonbeam. I'm pretty sure that Donny will confirm that the dust came from emeralds and that the prints that you brought in will not match any EMT's, officers' or ours, but there's still something that doesn't seem right. This whole problem isn't easy. Maybe Moonbeam can shed a new light on the picture?"

Bill puts down the pen and looks up, "How? I don't think so. Honestly Mariah, I'm doing this to make you feel better! I left the cane out of the mix for now but I have second thoughts. It should go back to Donny as soon as we're done here."

Mariah is persistent, "Bill if it makes you feel more secure, come with me so we can make sure that the evidence is properly handled. Moonbeam really might surprise you. I know that I doubted her in the past. But I have to admit, she has been right about Jocko. You know, people trust her with all kinds of things."

Bill sits back in the booth, "Mariah there were so many different prints I almost think I put up tape that reads 'Parade In Progress' by error. Someone wanted the emeralds; it was a crime of greed simple as that. You really read too much into things. Taggert's wife is Jocko's ex. There's motive if she knew about his secret and let's not forget about your visitors. What were their names Passo or Pesto or Pablo and Anna? Sounds like a fun Mexican bar... Pacco and Anna's."

Mariah interjects, "First of all Bill, you know nothing about women. Anna loved Jocko; you could tell by her letters. Pacco was Jocko's right hand man. It has got to be someone else... I can feel it and maybe Moonbeam can too."

By now, Bill's arms are crossed. He senses that he may not win this one. "Mariah why bother doing lab tests. Why not hold the cane in the air close your eyes and guess. That's how you want me to handle the case. You're unbelievable! Who died and made you police chief?"

"Well no-one did, but you remember how sweet Jocko was to Moonbeam. He took an interest in her talent. I'm sure he would approve. Please come with me and listen to what she has to say. Just Listen. It can't hurt and the chief is not going to be charged. My store will pay her bill if she even insists on one. What do you say?"

Bill uncrosses his arms. He sees the smile on Mariah's face as he looks at her sternly, "Well if any debt is picked up by your store I guess it wouldn't hurt. Go ahead give her a call but she has to come to the cane. She has to meet us at Jocko's tomorrow morning Tell her that it has to stay wrapped in plastic."

"Oh Bill," Mariah croons, "You are the most forward thinking policeman in the world. I promise you'll not regret this. I promise." Mariah is so excited; she gets up quickly and leaves before her dinner comes. She wants to call Moonbeam before Bill changes his mind. She runs outside to the payphone. It's dark. She hears a heavy rustling in the bushes but doesn't pay any attention thinking that the noise is a big old hungry raccoon scampering off. Something or rather someone does scamper off, not wanting to be identified.

Mariah knows Moonbeam's number by heart; she puts her quarter in the slot and begins to dial 221-MOON. She listens as the phone rings four times. Mariah is anxious for friend to pick up.

CHAPTER TWENTY-ONE
MOONBEAM'S RESIDENCE

To the ordinary eye, Moonbeam and Mariah may seem like unlikely friends but they really do have a great deal in common. They each opened their respective businesses at the same time. Moonbeam transformed herself six years ago, the same year that Mariah opened her popular shop. Each business in its own way contributes to the unique flavor of this little island.

Close in age, Mariah is thirty-eight; Moonbeam is thirty-six, both are very attractive in strikingly different ways. Of course, Mariah would want to consult Moonbeam because they are best friends and her advice is not considered psychic but trusted.

Both women are shopkeepers, catering to the massive tourist trade that hits this bucolic island every season. Moonbeam closes up shop a bit earlier than Mariah and frequently drops by in the evening for a movie and a chat. They commiserate about grumpy customers and laugh at the day's mishaps.

Through many hours of commiserating and laughs, the two became instant friends. Mariah is an island native who returned to her roots. Moonbeam is a transplant from the cold winds of Chicago. Her ancestral roots are native tracing right back to this area of Florida and the Micosukee Tribe. Her ancestors on her mother's side date back to the founding tribes in the Southwest Florida area. This part of her family tree served as the draw that made Moonbeam choose Seabliss over other areas of the state.

Moonbeam's first visit to Seabliss was twofold: to get away from the stress surrounding the world of commodities trading and to trace her family tree since Seabliss is not far from the Micosukee Reservation. The more she visited; the more she fell in love with the history of the area as well as the relaxed island lifestyle. After making a not too difficult decision to move, she decided to change careers and opened her shop as a hobby. She had enough money saved to coast for a while so she intended to do just that.

"I now have the luxury to examine my own feelings about the spiritual world." She explains, "Once I opened these doors to my own past, I found that I could no longer close or ignore them."

Yes she does have blond (well, really light brown) hair and the last name of Bromley, but after researching her family tree, she learns that English, Nordic and Micosukee blood flow equally through her veins. Her great-great grandmother on her mother's side was a spiritual healer for her tribe and communicator with the dead. "How beautiful" Moonbeam always thought, "And how lucky I am to have this deep connection with nature." The more Moonbeam learned about her great-great grandmother, the more serious she became about harnessing her inner powers. She learned that her ancestor possessed the power to warn her tribe about approaching enemies, to heal with herbs, and to channel the tribe's past elders for advice.

Moonbeam has been told by others with the gift that psychic powers skip a generation before being passed on. She is the right generation. As Moonbeam starts to believe in herself, she builds on her own psychic abilities. Sure she sells necklaces and puts on a show for tourists, but beneath all of the hype and the desire to earn money lies a deep and respectful connection with the spiritual world.

When Mrs. Dotley came in for advise about taking a bus trip to St. Augustine, Moonbeam closed her eyes and saw a rim without a tire in a ditch by the side of the road. She advised the older woman not to go. That next weekend the same bus that Mrs. Dotley was supposed to ride blew out a front tire on the way and ended up in a ditch. Because of the speed of travel, many of the passengers were injured and taken to local hospitals. The rest of the trip was cancelled.

Moonbeam inherited her great great grandmother's eyes, dark, round and very penetrating. Even with a few signs of middle age, Moonbeam is still very beautiful and very exotic. Her dress adds to her mystery with long and colorful gauze skirts, white gypsy-like blouses and of course bright pink, lavender and green scarves tying her waist-length hair back. It did not take long for Catherine May Bromley to become Moonbeam. Soon after she became friends with a local Micosukee spiritual guide named Gray Eagle. He became her teacher regarding the different tribes in the area and their amazing healing powers. He also was the one who chose "Moonbeam" as her new Americanized spiritual name.

He saw that Catherine has a round face with skin as smooth as silk. "Your face is round like the full moon," Gray Eagle used to tell her. "And your eyes sparkle like beams of light projecting from its surface. You are my Moonbeam." The name fit and therefore it stuck. No more Catherine, no more spread sheets. Moonbeam opened her shop full time in a little island cottage on a side street just off of the small main shopping and eating district. Since her business is based on word of mouth, she does not need a prime location just one that is zoned properly. Moonbeam is the only practicing psychic on Seabliss. There are others with her senses that also reside on the island but they wish to remain private. When Moonbeam has trouble using her gift, she calls on one of the others for advice. They are always glad to oblige her.

Moonbeam's place of business is also her residence. It is a peach colored cottage, the second house in on the street with a sign the shape of a hibiscus that reads simply "PSYCHIC." She has many repeat customers as well as visitors hoping to hear good news. Moonbeam has not lost her business skills. She reads the island hotel front desk clerks for free so that they will refer business her way. Since she is the only practicing psychic on Seabliss; her services are in demand. Over the years, Moonbeam has developed quite a loyal local following with some of her patrons coming from the mainland and other islands. Her shop sells herbs and beautiful crystals, oils, candles and books pertaining to matters of the spirit. It sells enough merchandise to give Moonbeam a steady income so that she can continue to learn about her spiritual powers. Her reputation for helping resolve marital problems, insomnia, weight loss and other personal issues is well known. The world of crime which she is soon about to enter, however, is something very new and different for her.

Moonbeam is in the middle of a reading when the phone rings. She does evening readings for her clients who work or don't want to hire babysitters. She is concentrating so intently that the actual ring makes her jump. Moonbeam's assistant and long-time advisor Gray Eagle answers the phone "Cosmic Cottage"

"Hey Gray Bird. It's Mariah. Where's Moonie?"

The Eagle hates when Mariah calls him that. He remains composed so as to protect his image in front of a customer. "Madame, Moonbeam is in an important reading. I am not allowed to interfere."

Mariah pauses for a second, "Well, Birdie, tell Madame her services are required for police business. Tell her it's official and that we're coming over right now to ask for her services."

By now, Gray Eagle has a look of complete terror come over his face. He is a Virgo and everything has to be orderly. "Mariah you know better than that. No jokes, She's with a client"

"This is no Joke!" Mariah chirps in, "I'm with the assistant police chief, so tell her to get ready for our visit. As a newly appointed deputy I must warn you that you may be interfering with an on-going investigation. Thanks and Toodles." With that Mariah hangs up.

Gray Eagle puts the receiver down and grabs a piece of notepaper. He hastily writes a note to Moonbeam and places it in a silver foil envelope. He goes back into the reading room and passes the note to Moonbeam whose eyes are closed in concentration. Moonbeam slowly opens her eyes, dramatically opens the envelope and reads the scribbled message. When she finishes, she puts her hands over her eyes and shakes her head. "I am terribly sorry, Mrs. Baxter, but something of the most urgent nature has come to my attention. Someone in the Great Beyond is in dire need of my services and I must assist. This reading must come to a close. I owe you five minutes so next week I will add fifteen to your time. Gray Eagle, please make a note by Mrs. Baxter's appointment as a reminder. I am grateful for your understanding," Moonbeam has a very soothing voice; that is one reason that she is so popular with her clients. The other reason is that she is accurate. She has inherited a very special talent and she does not sense how powerful her talent really is.

The customer nods and leaves happy. Eagle thinks Moonbeam must have given her good news. Moonbeam is just about to take a well-deserved break when the phone rings again. She answers the phone herself, "Feel your inner strength, feel the wind."

"OK, you can officially cut the crap. Moonbeam this is Mariah. Can you meet us at Jocko's tomorrow at nine A.M. to read his cane?"

Moonbeam is stunned. "Read his cane…Tomorrow…but why…Do you think it will help us find out what happened to him?"

Mariah responds quickly.

"Yep, besides you may be the only one who has what it takes to find his murderer. I'm convinced that whoever murdered Jocko also touched his cane. I need to know everything about this person." Mariah sounds firm.

"Well," Moonbeam is a bit defiant, "It can't be crap or you wouldn't ask me to do this. I will but, as you insulted my senses, I will do it as a favor for Jocko, not for you!"

There is an awkward moment of silence. Moonbeam's business powers now take center stage. She's always looking to make a few extra bucks. "Mariah, tell the chief, you know my services are not cheap."

"Moonie, this is for us, for Jocko. Think of this as your big chance to perform a community service. That same community that has supported you since you arrived here. I know that you will do the right thing. Who knows your story may even end up on TV on one of those crime channels. You might even end up with your own show."

"Besides, if you cannot do it for free, I will personally pay you. I need this done for Jocko." Moonbeam listens quietly. She knows how much Mariah loved Jocko. She wants to help Mariah and would never make her friend pay. "OK Mariah, community service it is. I'll be there first thing in the morning."

Moonbeam then picks up her purse from her desk and instructs the Eagle, "No appointments tomorrow until after three, please reschedule anything that might interfere. I have an appointment that could easily keep me busy into tomorrow afternoon." She turns the OPEN sign to read CLOSED, wishes The Eagle a good night and heads for her living quarters.

Nine A.M. comes early. Moonbeam finishes her herbal tea and waits for Gray Eagle. As soon as he arrives, she lifts the solid brass latch that opens the front door. "I'm leaving now. Wish me luck."

Gray Eagle is quick to respond, "Those with the gift do not need luck."

With that, Moonbeam closes the door and heads for Jocko's.

Bill picks Mariah up at her store. He has the cane with him. Bill has secretly kept the cane locked in the evidence locker overnight especially since Donnie confirmed the presence of emeralds in the secret compartment.

At almost the exact time that Moonbeam leaves her cottage for Jocko's, a man dressed in black comes out from a small hut near a concrete commercial building well hidden in thick tropical brush not too far outside of Seabliss. "Are they ready to go?," he asks. The two men in a truck respond, "They are all set. Your TVs are ready to load on the trucks now."

"Good," the man says, "The boss will be pleased. Load them now."

As the last box is loaded, the man in black, stiffens, thanks his workers and then fires two quick well placed shots to the head killing both men. He looks back at the hut. "Hugo come out here, I think it's time to feed these gators."

CHAPTER TWENTY-TWO

"Jocko is that you? "As soon as Moonbeam steps foot on Jocko's condo parking lot, she feels a sudden gust of cold wind blowing through her hair even though the thermometer reads eighty-five. "I hate to be the one to tell you 'I told you so', but I warned you the last time I did a reading for you." Moonbeam waves her finger in the morning air as if scolding the spirit. She is proud of the fact that she has always been discreet about Jocko's readings, as he didn't want anyone to know.

"I warned you and you just shrugged it off. How I wish you had listened to me. We wouldn't be standing here now. I promise that I'll do my best to listen to whatever you have to tell me. I'll communicate your deepest feelings to Mariah and Bill so that your spirit can be at peace."

As she finishes her peculiar conversation, she finds herself at the foot of the stairs leading up to the Captain's apartment. She practically runs up the stairs knowing that Mariah and Bill are probably waiting anxiously

As she approaches Jocko's front door, she sees that they have left it open for her. She sticks her head around the doorframe, "Hello Bill? Mariah anybody here?'

She does not want to cross the yellow tape unless Bill okays it.

"Hey Moonbeam, come on in, we're over here." Bill shouts from the kitchen. Moonbeam enters cautiously. She stands in the doorway with her eyes closed and head lifted toward the sky. One hand is over her head. She turns around making a circle. "Jocko is here. I can feel him. He wants you to know that I have been selected to channel his thoughts and feelings. "She then opens her eyes and looks at Bill standing in a pose of disbelief with his arms folded. "Moonbeam that's all well and good sweetie, but this is a police investigation and we run on science, what little we have here in Seabliss. This whole cane deal is Mariah's idea. Remember if you have a bill, send it to her at the video store. The chief doesn't recognize channeling as a regular department expense."

Moonbeam steps a little closer to the chair where they found Jocko. "Moonbeam, we carefully placed the cane exactly where it was when we found him." Mariah instructs her," I hope that helps."

"Hey Mariah, good job, I must be starting to rub off on you." As she approaches the chair, however, her face becomes very somber. "This is terrible. How could anyone do something as awful as this to such a sweet old man?" Bill, who is always skeptical of Moonbeam's talent, takes her to the side of the chair nearest the cane. "Well, Houdini, there's your magic wand. Tell us all that you know."

Moonbeam shrugs off Bill's attempt at humor. "Thanks Bill, but I have a somber job to perform. I have to do it properly to help Jocko." She becomes very quiet, very intense as she lifts the cane and holds it up to her eyes. She then closes her eyes and begins to gently stroke the bagged cane in a slow methodical manner from one side to the other. She takes a deep breath. Bill and Mariah are speechless. What is she trying to accomplish? Moonbeam then lifts the cane over her head holding it in both hands. She speaks softly in what appears to be a chant.

Moonbeam is silent for a few minutes as if waiting for something. "I really couldn't tell you much now. I guess I'm not quite in tune. I can try holding the cane again and concentrating on Jocko again. I sense that many people are involved with the cane especially two women. They were both very close to Jocko. One came through with cold vibes; the other mixed. One is either a relative or a former friend, the other a lover. The male vibes are not as strong. I'll try once more."

Moonbeam then regains her composure, takes a deep breath and carefully picks up the cane and lifts it above her head. "Abu, Abu, spiritu summon," She repeats her command three times. The higher she lifts the cane, the tighter she closes her eyes. Moonbeam begins to tremble and tremble until her trembling turns into a violent shaking. She starts to moan very weakly and slowly as if in pain. Bill stands as still as a statue watching; even Mariah is silent with her mouth wide open. Mariah shakes Bill, "Pay attention, she may go into convulsions," she whispers as quietly as she can. "We must wake her gently." Bill approaches Moonbeam very slowly and gently touches her shoulder. As if instantaneous, Moonbeam drops the cane as quickly as Bill touches her. Just then the shaking stops. Moonbeam falls to the floor and opens her eyes. She takes a deep gasp for air before speaking. "The spirit Abu who guides the dead tells me that five people all with bad intentions have touched this cane besides Jocko. Three are men and two are women. The murderer is among them. The color green is important and the crime is one of envy."

Bill breaks the silence first; one that is so thick you cold cut it with a knife. "Well, Moonie, you don't have to be Dick Tracey to know most of that."

Mariah is perturbed, "Bill why don't you just shut up. Moonbeam may be on to something that we didn't know. Five evil people touched the cane. That excludes you and me, but not Pacco and Anna." The fifth person is a man. Moonbeam, what can you tell us about the fifth person?"

"Fifth person? Who the hell are one through four?" Bill asks.

"He belongs to them, "Moonbeam cryptically answers.

"He belongs to who?" Bill asks.

"I'm not exactly sure," Moonbeam continues, "I must hold the cane one more time to be absolutely sure."

Bill opens one arm and points to where the cane landed after her trance. "Well there is your magic wand. So go for it."

Moonbeam has to totally ignore Bill's wise remarks. She is professional and extremely serious about her craft. She is determined to help her friend find Jocko's killer as well as to find peace for Jocko's soul.

Moonbeam gets up and slowly walks around the chair. Bill and Mariah remain perfectly silent.

After what happened during the last cane holding, they don't know what to expect now. The only sound in the room is Moonbeam's jingling ankle bracelets and earrings. She circles the chair one more time and stops. Moonbeam gently picks up the beautifully carved wrapped cane with her right hand. She closes her eyes and slowly strokes the side of the cane with her left hand. She feels the cane on one side then touches the other. Then placing both hands on the exact middle of the cane, she slowly lifts it over her head. She mutters her incantation again quietly, "Abu, Abu spirit shine." Simultaneously, a cold gust of wind rushes through Mariah and Bill giving them a chill. They say nothing but the look in their eyes says it all. When the wind passes, Moonbeam starts to shake again. She is shaking so hard that she is vibrating. As Bill watches, he thinks, "It's a good act, no wonder she gets big bucks from the tourists."

Mariah also watches in silence. Her eyes are not just fixated on Moonbeam but on the cane in the hopes that it will reveal clues, any kind of clues.

Moonbeam's convulsive shaking eases as her right hand comes off of the cane first. She opens her eyes as if awakening from a trance. "Abu says again that three men and two women who are all envious of Jocko have touched this cane. His death the spirit repeats is a cold blooded murder of envy."

"Well I don't need a psychic to figure this out, "Bill chimes in. "Shut up Bill," Mariah scolds, "Let her finish OK? If Moonbeam is right, two of our suspects may have already been accounted for. Moonbeam what can you tell us about the people who last touched this cane?"

Moonbeam pauses. She holds the cane with her right arm. "One of the women was very close to him like a lover or former lover. The men do not know each other very well. Let me try one more time to see what the cane tells me about the men." Moonbeam grabs onto the cane with both hands. She once again lifts it into the air. Closing her eyes, she repeats, "Abu, Abu spirit shine." Almost at once she starts to tremble, then shake and then vibrate. She shook more violently then before. She starts to moan, "Oooooooooooooo." Her moaning is slow almost like a person in pain.

Mariah is watching in disbelief. Bill is skeptical but intent on seeing what Moonbeam will do next. Moonbeam's moans and convulsive shaking continue only to become louder and more violent. Mariah becomes concerned. "Quick Bill, wake her up."

Bill gives Mariah a quick smug look but being the gentleman that he is plays along with the whole thing. He gently touches Moonbeam's arm like the last time but that does not work. He touches her shoulder and then decides to pull one arm off of the cane. Oddly, it is a struggle for Bill to get Moonbeam's grasp free of the cane. She wakes up startled and out of breath. She jumps at the sight of Mariah and Bill.

"We are dealing with bad people. All of them are very bad.' She says quickly her eyes filled with fear. "One is filled with envy; another deep in crime, the others greed. All have many secrets. Jocko knew some of these secrets. That is something that they didn't like."

Mariah listens carefully trying to absorb Moonbeam's interpretation of the crime. "Moonbeam, the one filled with crime, are these crimes in the present or past?"

Moonbeam looks at her with a most serious gaze. She answers slowly, "Present. Bad, bad things." Moonbeam's facial expressions convey fear and stress. "I can feel his presence." Just as she speaks those words, the trio hears the sound of heavy footsteps approaching the door making all of them jump.

Mariah looks at the entranceway to see a tall well-tanned man, very lean and very well dressed. She is looking straight into the eyes but does not know who he is. As she looks deep into his eyes, she wonders if someone so handsome could be the evil that Moonbeam mentions. Mariah is the first one to approach him. Moonbeam steps back as if in fear making Bill put his hand on his gun.

Mariah quickly glances over at Moonbeam whose face is filled with total fear. Hoping to break the tension, she greets the stranger, "By all means, please come in."

Bill is less fearful but far less cordial. "Grand Central Station. Next stop Jocko's. Where do all these damn people come from?"

Mariah smiles almost flirting with the handsome stranger. He smiles back flashing a gold tooth under a well-groomed black mustache. "May I come in? I wish to pay my respects," he asks politely. Moonbeam is still not impressed but Mariah, who is curious to the hilt, responds, "Please come in. Do you mind if I ask your name and how you knew Jocko? My name is Mariah. I was a good friend of his and you are?"

CHAPTER TWENTY-THREE

Those same island breezes that blow cold at Jocko's are now warm and gentile as they waft through the open patio restaurant of the Sandbarre. Locals and tourists are laughing as they enjoy their pina coladas and frozen margaritas talking about their day's fun activities over lunch. Doc, on the other hand, is very quiet and sitting alone at a table off to one corner. He is still drowning out the haunting memories of his only autopsy with his favorite single malt scotch, Glenfiddich.

By now, Doc is wondering where Moonbeam is. "She promised that she would meet me here. I've called her at work, at Mariah's but I just can't seem to track her down. She always breaks for lunch."

Doc is a popular guy but he is really lost without Moonbeam. After downing two shots of scotch, he decides to leave. He asks the regular server to tell Moonbeam that he left. "She'll know where to look next. After all, there are only so many bars on the island." He decides to bide his time by frequenting another local watering hole "The Silver Mermaid."

This bar is aptly named because of the large concentration of shells beneath the clear water of its shoreline that sparkle silver in the sun. The Silver Mermaid is housed in a yellow building with a wrap around porch hosting incredible views of the Gulf. The island's founding fathers, really pirates, believed that mermaids swam in the warm Gulf waters near this specific spot. They actually did see large creatures with rounded tails off the coast but after all the rum they imbibed, their minds turned manatees into mermaids. So when brothers Rod and Tim Jensen opened their popular pub, they agreed that some kind of historical reference was in order since the pirates were probably drunk out of their minds anyway.

In keeping with pub traditions, Rod and Tim realized that the pirates had to be three sheets to the wind to make such a mistake and figured that this spot might have been the first "watering hole" on the island. They thus added a touch of history to their bar with a good story that works wonders with the tourists.

As Doc enters, his eyes wander around the patio; all he sees are happy people. All he hears is their loud laughter. He notices an extremely beautiful Latino woman sitting at the outside bar alone and quiet. She like him looks sad, very sad. Since the bar is not far from where he normally sits, he can hear her conversation with the bartender. He hears her order a Margarita and then confides to the bartender, "I'm so depressed. I just lost the best friend that I ever had. He was the love of my life. I don't know how I can live without him. Perhaps you knew him? Captain Jocko?"

For Doc, just hearing Jocko's name brings back the horrible images of his autopsy. He orders his favorite scotch straight up with water on the side. He believes his drink to be a medicinal necessity. He gulps it down, then orders a less expensive blended scotch to sip. He sits back in his chair trying not to pay attention to all of the comings and goings of the patrons, but that one beautiful yet unfamiliar woman piques his imagination. An air of mystery surrounds her as she sadly lights up a cigarette and orders another Margarita. Tears begin to swell in her eyes. She slowly swivels her barstool to face the water. As she does, her eyes meet Doc's. She wants him to notice her. She wants him to talk to her.

Doc is drawn in like a fly to a spider. He gets up and sits down on the stool next to hers. "Excuse me, I don't mean to pry but I couldn't help overhearing your conversation. I knew Jocko as well. I was his doctor. I'm Doctor Tranor. Doc for short and you are?"

The woman looks up at Doc with enormous almond brown eyes and says quietly, "Anna, I am Anna. Jocko and I are…were partners in a pottery factory in Mexico. He so wanted to retire there and now this has to happen."

Her large brown eyes gaze deeply into Doc's. Could she be Doc's mermaid? Doc never wanting to see a damsel in distress, offers her his handkerchief and says, "Again, I don't mean to pry but you were close to the Captain?' The woman starts to cry again, this time into Doc's handkerchief, "Oh, he was more than a partner, he was the love of my life, my best friend."

She looks up, "My life will never be the same without my Captain Jocko." Doc is more than surprised. First of all, Jocko never mentioned that he had any "Love of his life" let alone one so lovely and secondly sorry that he asked because he did not want to tell her that he performed the autopsy. He pauses,

"Yes, Jocko was a good man. We all thought a great deal of him."

"Oh I am sorry to cry," she responds delicately, "But. Jocko and I have been together for a long time. We built a business in Mexico together. Maybe he told you about it? That's why he came to Mexico so often. The one time that I come to surprise him, I come to learn of his death."

She starts sobbing again. "There, there now, my dear" Doc says trying to calm her down." Are you staying on the island?"

"Yes I am at The Blue Heron Inn. I will be leaving though in a few days after Jocko's funeral. I do not know when it is but I must stay to arrange it and bring my Captain home. There are others from my village here as well." With that the beautiful woman opens a small black clutch purse and hands Doc her card. Before doing so she writes her local address and extension at the Inn.

Doc gulps down the rest of his scotch. He pulls his business card holder from his pocket and gives her one. Holding her hand, he tells her, " I am deeply sorry for your loss. If there is anyway I can be of assistance here is my number." He hands the card to the woman, pays for their drinks and then leaves to look for Moonbeam.

CHAPTER TWENTY-FOUR

The handsome dark stranger at Jocko's flashes another charming smile for Mariah and then begins to speak. Moonbeam won't let herself be taken in by his charm. Right now, the psychic is up to her ears in intrigue and at a loss for words. She stands back at a safe distance, just staring at Mariah and the mystery man.

The man's voice is deep and smooth, "Excuse me Senora, as I stated I am trying to find out where they took Captain Jocko's remains. Can you tell me where to find him?" The stranger walks out of the doorway and out of the shadows. He becomes visible to all. Mariah is the only one brave enough to take the initiative and walk toward him. "After all," she thinks, "I've already met two other friends of Jocko's and I'm still here."

The man enters the room and walks toward her. He is so striking that it would be hard for any normal woman to ignore his good looks, but Mariah is on a mission. Moonbeam, on the other hand, has her eyes closed hoping to silently ward off evil. She grabs onto Jocko's cane tightly as a measure of self-defense in both the spiritual and the physical sense.

"Excuse me ladies and gentleman," nodding to Bill, "My name is Alejandro. I am a Jocko's son and I have come to pay my respects. I don't know where they have brought his body. I have come here to the place where he died in the hopes of getting that information."

As Alejandro speaks, Moonbeam opens her eyes wide. She is definitely awake. Her previous words echo in her mind. "Two of the men are bad—one is very bad. All are envious; one is filled with crime and one has secrets he does not want revealed." Moonbeam knows that Jocko knew their secrets and they didn't like that. Moonbeam wonders, "Could Jocko's own son be one of them?"

Alejandro looks very sad and somewhat uncomfortable. Mariah tries to put him at ease. "I'm so sorry for your loss. The Captain was a good man and a good friend. I was a very close friend of your father's."

Alejandro looks surprised at this last statement.

His grief appears to prompt the following questions. "When?...How?...What happened?"

"Please come in to the living room with me, "she tells him. "That is where Jocko died." She points to the chair.

Bill is not as much afraid as annoyed that Mariah would just open up at a crime scene to a total stranger with no identification.

"Damn Grand Central Station. Sure come on in…let me give you the two dollar tour. How many more can we squeeze in here Mariah?"

Mariah ignores Bill's seemingly rude remarks. As the man enters the room, Moonbeam approaches him slowly and cautiously. She looks into his eyes, smiles while methodically grabbing onto his arm. "And, may I ask, when did you see Jocko last? I'm also his friend."

Alejandro's name has a musical ring to Mariah's ears; Bill can sense that she is drawn in by his charm.

"Certainly, madam, I'm sorry I did not get your name," looking directly at Moonbeam." It has been a few months since our last visit, but he knows that I am always in his life. Jocko was a good father and a true friend to all."

"My name is Moonbeam. Your father was a friend of mine as well." Moonbeam tears up as she puts Alejandro's hands in hers. "He's a hard man to replace. I never met anyone else like him."

"Senorita, I am as sorry for your loss as mine. We shared the friendship and love of a great man. Jocko and I lived in the same small Mexican village. I also know his love, Anna and his worker Pacco. I understand that she and Pacco came here to see you as well." He looks over at Mariah who winces as Bill gives her a look. Moonbeam also looks at Mariah. They share the same secret thought. Alejandro could be the third man in Moonie's prediction.

Moonbeam is still holding onto his arm. She feigns a smile as she hopes to read him without causing too much suspicion. The mystery man smiles back and Moonbeam gently lets go. She couldn't get a clear reading; she knows that she has to try again.

Moonbeam desperately wants to feel his aura. She positions herself closer to the man again. She reaches out and touches his arm again as if to console him.

"Alejandro, May I show you around Jocko's apartment?" Moonbeam walks him by Jocko's chair. Still holding onto his arm, she points to the cane. By now, she has returned it to its original position of leaning against the side of the chair. His eyes focus on that one object and that one object only. Alejandro cannot stop staring at it and seems deaf to the conversations around him. He leans down to touch it but Mariah stops him. "That's still police evidence. It's wrapped in plastic. Please don't touch it."

Moonbeam walks with him into the kitchen. "I can feel how deep your loss is. If you'd like to look around, I would be delighted to show you the rest his home." As Moonbeam speaks to him, she puts her other hand on his arm hoping that two hands will increase her spiritual flow.

As soon as her other hand touches his arm, Moonbeam actually begins to pick up some vibes. She hopes to hold onto him for a few more seconds to determine what they mean.

"I remember," he starts to speak, "that Jocko carried a cane with him at all times. When you can give away his possessions, may I have the cane as a remembrance of him? It would mean a great deal to me. I would treasure it." Moonbeam is silent but Mariah responds quickly, "I'm sure you would as we all would. It was very special to Jocko but for now it stays here. It's too soon to think of things like that."

Alejandro grabs Moonbeam's hand and removes it from his arm just before she can clearly read him.

"Yes I understand. Please remember that I would like to have it very much. I remember how much he enjoyed walking with that cane. It is as if he is with us now." Moonbeam cannot help but thinking, "He sure is Bud." Moonbeam continues the tour heading for the bedroom; Mariah follows close behind. They both sense how much Alejandro's eyes scan the combined kitchen and living room.

After his tour of the apartment, he walks slowly back to the front door. "I must go now. Again, I need to know where my father has been taken. Thank you for your concern."

Mariah answers softly, "Jocko is with the medical examiner pending the results of tests and also pending notification of his next of kin."

"Jocko has no next of kin besides myself that is. We were very close," Alejandro responds, "Please call me so I know when I can plan his funeral. Tell me then when I can pick up his cane and other things. I am staying at the Twin Palm Inn if I can be of any assistance. Until then Adios."

"Adios Alejandro. I will call you when we decide to give Jocko's things away." Mariah sounds assuring. Alejandro takes his leave. When they hear his footsteps reach the bottom step and are sure that he is not within earshot, Bill is the first to speak." Mariah what do you mean when WE start giving away Jocko's things? First of all, how do we know that Alejandro is the next of kin and secondly dammit this is a crime scene not an auction. Everything right now is evidence and, remember ladies, you are not judge and jury. There are laws. If Alejandro is really Jocko's son, we require proof like a birth certificate before he gets anything."

Bill has remained speechless through most of this unusual visit. He sure isn't now. "What do you two amateurs think you are doing? That cane is police evidence and it is not I repeat not going anywhere. The disposition of the cane is not for you to even discuss!"

Mariah chimes in, "I know that and you know that but he doesn't know you can't release it. I feel like a spider, the cane is my web and Alejandro is a fly." Mariah laughs "Cool it Bill, we have to know more about this guy. He seems real interested in the cane. Maybe he doesn't know that the valuables are gone from the cane? Or maybe he took them and is trying to throw us off his scent? At any rate you can catch more flies with honey."

Moonbeam remains quiet. She closes her eyes and crosses her arms. She hums gently and whispers some odd words.

"The spirit senses that one very bad man has left our presence."

With that Moonbeam goes into the bedroom hoping to sense more.

Just then, the remaining two are interrupted again by a knock coming from the front entrance. Mariah turns around to see Pacco. "Excuse me madam, I wanted you to know that I telephoned the pottery factory and told them the sad news about Senor Jocko, They know that Anna would like to take Jocko's ashes home. She will call them soon with a request to make special funeral urns to transport Jocko's remains to Mexico. I thought that you should know."

Mariah is stunned to see the short man again. Bill is matter of fact." Jocko is at the morgue waiting autopsy results and then proof of next of kin." Mariah is quiet. Moonbeam is still in the bedroom unaware of Pacco's visit.

Pacco continues, "Anna would like to claim him since they were like husband and wife for over twenty years so I will be in touch." With that the short stocky Pablo turns and leaves.

Moonbeam suddenly bursts out of the other room grabbing her throat as if she is being choked. "Alejandro is evil. I can feel it. We should definitely follow him."

Bill wants to put a cork in all of this amateur sleuthing right now. "OK ladies let's lock it up here. You two go back and take care of your businesses and leave the detective work to my guys and me. Moonbeam, I bet there's a client just waiting on your porch. Mariah, I bet at least ten disasters have occurred at your store without you. So let's all go back to normal. Agreed?" Bill looks at the two women sternly as he picks up the bagged cane to bring it back to the crime lab.

The two women look at each other smiling. Mariah uses their secret hand signal. She places her right hand on her left wrist and holds it. They devised this form of communication to help leave boring town events together without being noticed to talk about what they heard or saw. Sometimes that can actually be more fun.

"Agreed." They answer simultaneously not meaning a word of it. Bill appears to be a bit calmer, "May I give you lovely ladies a lift back to work?' I am heading in your direction." Again almost simultaneously, the two women respond, "No we like to walk. We'll see you around Bill."

All three leave Jock's apartment; Bill locks the front door. They walk slowly down the steps. Each of them is deep in his or her own thoughts. Bill gets into his patrol car and waves goodbye. Mariah and Moonbeam nod trying not to show how anxious they are to plan a secret field trip to the Twin Palm Inn.

CHAPTER TWENTY-FIVE

Giggling like a pair of teen-age school chums who just got way with something, Mariah and Moonbeam stand in front of Mariah's store plotting their next move. Moonbeam begins sounding quite serious. "We both trust what the cane revealed to us, but we know we need to learn more. The Twin Palm Inn is not that far away from us but going there unnoticed makes it seem like light years away. How do you think we should proceed?"

Mariah and Moonbeam go into the store to discuss privately the best way to approach this. They enter Mariah's small office and close the door hoping that no one has paid attention to their arrival. That, however, is not the case as they soon hear a whimper. It's Spike who does not like being left out. He pushes the unlocked door open and bolts in practically sitting on their laps.

"Well, Moonie, my guess is that Bill might want to go to Jocko's one more time. I will go with him to see if we can piece the crime scene together using the info from your reading. If Alejandro is as evil as you say, we may have to approach the search from a different angle. You were great by the way. Jocko would have been proud."

"Thanks, Mariah. I miss Jocko. This whole thing makes me very sad but I know we have to stay with it. His killers are still here; I can feel them. Maybe I can sneak over to the Inn to learn more while you keep Bill occupied."

"It's so much fun fooling Bill," Mariah smiles, "I love the thought that little old us may have the upper hand on the case."

"Hey Mariah," Moonbeam starts to laugh." Why don't we tell Bill that we all need to go to Jocko's to do a séance to see who in Jocko's past may have caused this present woe?"

Mariah sits back as if interested. "Good thinking, but can we sell it to Bill?"

"Mariah, there's nothing to sell. I would really do one. It may help. Really. Trust me, I do this all of the time."

"I would love to see the look on his face," Mariah chirps in, "But I'll do anything to catch the killer. OK you're on. You go home and rest up. Leave our Mr. Bill to me."

The two friends hug. "Our hug," Moonbeam begins, "Solidifies our desire to help Jocko by whatever means necessary. I have a secret to share with you. Jocko tried to communicate with me again before I went up to his apartment. We need to hold a séance there. I know that he will come back to me."

"What did you say? Jocko tried to communicate with you again? For real?" Mariah is stunned by this news. "I need to talk to Bill. He has to cooperate. Jocko himself may tell us who killed him!"

They get up and leave the office. Moonbeam heads for home.

Mariah goes back to work at the counter as if energized by a special force.

Spike follows her breathing a deep sigh.

CHAPTER TWENTY-SIX

The next day, Moonbeam finds herself in the midst of a very slow business cycle. The sun is shining brightly on Seabliss giving the Gulf waters a sparkling emerald glow. The mild island breezes are refreshing. This unbeatable combination makes for the perfect beach day. A perfect beach day like today is the magnet that draws tourists and nearby locals to the island. Unfortunately, when they need a break from the sun, they tend to frequent the bars and restaurants. Psychic readings do much better on a gray day.

Today, since Moonbeam's walk-in business is non-existent, she decides to catch up on some much needed rest. Trying to track down a killer can drain a psychic spiritually. She has had a few restless nights for no apparent reason except for some very odd dreams.

Moonbeam makes a cup of herbal tea to calm her frazzled nerves and slips off her sandals. Her cat Kira watches as Moonbeam snuggles into the cushioned window bench and pulls down the lavender ruffled shade. Once Moonbeam is lying down, Kira jumps on the bench and curls up on her lap. It does not take very long for the pair to fall asleep.

Moonbeam's sleep, however, is not the calm peaceful kind that she had hoped it would be. Her tired mind is working overtime. There are times that she does not really believe she has "the gift" even though others who know have witnessed it. Moonbeam remembers that her grandmother often reminded her that she was the true chosen one in her family. Some people may make fun of her profession, and she may have started "The Cosmic Cottage" to begin a new life, but one fact is indisputable, Moonbeam really does have "the gift."

Moonbeam starts to drift in and out of sleep and in the process can't stop tossing and turning. She is so restless that Kira can't stand it and jumps off of her lap for the pillow on the floor nearby. Moonbeam, still asleep, begins to scream. She becomes more restless as she dreams that she is on a Mexican beach where she meets two shadowy figures, one short and one tall. They are both dressed in black and their figures are ghost-like and blurry. Even though asleep, chills begin to roll up her spine. She feels as if she must flee them and she moves around so much that she almost falls off the window bench.

She cannot flee. They seem to follow her every move. Still dreaming she walks up to the tall one sensing that he is pure evil but being cosmically curious begins to talk to him anyway.

"Hello, do not go away. I am Moonbeam and want to learn why you have come to me in my dreams."

The man's face is partially blurred making his features undistinguishable. He begins to speak in a deep voice that sounds like a recording in slow speed.

"I will not tell you my name. I can tell you that I am coming to Seabliss to meet with some of your dearest friends. Once I leave, things will never be the same for you or any of them. If you know what is good for you, you will stay out of my way and will not warn your friends. Then I can spare you my wrath."

The short figure starts to approach her. His hands are gloved and outstretched as if to grab her neck.

Moonbeam screams again. This time, her screams wake her up in a start. "Who is this man? Is he real or is he my left over lunch talking? Why can't I tell anyone?"

Moonbeam can feel that her clothes are drenched with perspiration. She takes a deep breath and realizes that she has been given a message. She must collect her thoughts. "If I tell anyone besides Mariah, they will think that I've been drinking. I must find Mariah and tell her. One of the men may be Alejandro but who is the other one?"

Just as she gets up from of the window bench and combs her hair, she hears a knock at her door. Kira's fur is standing up straight as is her tail.

CHAPTER TWENTY-SEVEN

To add to Moonbeam's stress level, today is Gray Eagle's day off. Moonbeam has to open the door herself. She straightens her skirt, tosses her hair back quickly with her hands, and gives herself a quick dab of perfume so that she will appear presentable. Moonbeam sprays the room with her favorite fragrant frangipani scent quickly.

She looks for Kira. The cat is in the bedroom for some reason under the bed so Moonbeam closes that door and heads for the front door.

She says, "Coming" as this person knocks again. As she opens the door, she is surprised to see the man of her dreams. No not that kind of dream; the man who went for her throat. The short, stocky man dressed in black wearing a hat that covers his eyes.

"Senorita, may I come in." He speaks with a Spanish accent, perhaps she thinks Mexican. Moonbeam nods yes as she feels her pocket for her Swiss army knife. After all a girl can't be too careful in dealing with strangers.

The man steps across the threshold and looks side to side as if to see if anyone else is present. "I am told you have great powers. Powers that can even reach the dead. Is that true, my lady?"

Moonbeam is speechless as he continues. "I am told by one of your other clients that you can reach a certain sea captain. She told me this is so. I want to hire you. I need information on this man. I have even brought you an article of his clothing to hold."

Moonbeam senses evil; she also thinks that this man may be the one who ransacked Jocko's bedroom looking for something. How else could he have a piece of clothing?

"I hope I can help you, but my services are never exact. One must read as much into them as possible," she answers carefully.

"I understand," the short dark man responds. "I'm sure that you will do the best you can."

Moonbeam looks at his evil smile. The gold crowns in the front lower side make his thoughts glisten with wickedness.

"I might add that my services do not come cheap. I expect to be paid two hundred dollars for any special requests especially those concerning reaching the departed."

The man does not flinch. He reaches into his pocket and slowly pulls out his wallet. Moonbeam steps back a bit relieved that it isn't a gun. Her hand is in her pocket on her knife the whole time.

He opens his wallet and takes out two crisp one hundred dollar bills and hands them over to Moonbeam.

"Now let's get started. I have questions," the man says matter of factly.

"Please follow me," Moonbeam extends her arm as if to show the man into her center room that has a large round oak table with a crystal ball in the center of it.

"Please be seated, next to me if you don't mind." This way, the cunning Moonbeam may be able to read him as well. "Now, please give me the article of clothing as well as something of yours to gain the connection to the afterlife."

The man reaches in his other pocket and pulls out one of Jocko's favorite green ascots. He hands it over to Moonbeam who recognizes it immediately. She says nothing so as not to tip her hand. He then takes his hat off and hands that to her as well. Moonbeam now has a good look at his face.

Moonbeam's foot then hits a button under the table that shuts off the lights. She takes both articles of clothing and holds them up in the air. Her eyes closed, she invokes the spirits. "O mighty spirits from beyond please help me find the man who owns this scarf."

Her foot moves ever so quietly to another button; the table gently shakes as her crystal ball lights up. "Spirits I know that you can hear me. Answer me please. The man who owns this hat wants to know."

The man looks around at the table and the lit crystal ball wondering if this charlatan can really reach Jocko. His friend seems to think she can; because of that and only because of that, does he remains quiet.

"Please close your eyes and concentrate on the person you wish to contact."

Moonbeam instructs the stranger. The man unwillingly obliges. Moonbeam grabs his hand while holding the scarf and hat together in the other. Moonbeam feels something odd making her drop the hat. Her hand is locked around the scarf.

"Oh great spirits from the beyond. This man wishes to make contact. Please send a sign so we know that you can hear us!"

"Oh ! Ah!" Moonbeam moves quickly back in her chair as if taken by surprise. She yells as she opens her eyes to feel her hand burning. She looks over at it to see that the top of the ascot has caught on fire as if by spontaneous combustion. Quickly she gets up, runs into the kitchen and throws it in the sink pouring cold water all over it.

She stops for a few seconds surprised by her own skill while trying to see if the man is impressed.

"That's very odd," she thinks aloud as she re-enters the room. "I didn't see or smell you smoking. Could Jocko really be making contact with us?"

Moonbeam is now scaring herself. Maybe Jocko is trying to tell her not to communicate with that man. She must think of some way to get rid of him. This development is as surprising to Moonbeam as it is to her client.

She returns to her seat at the table. As quickly as she sits down, she feels a hand grabbing her neck from behind. She is scared and wants to open her mouth to ask for help, but the voice and the words that come out are not hers.

The voice is low and guttural. "The fire is from my belly. I no longer wish to communicate with you. I know that you have betrayed me, my fat money grubbing friend.'

With that last statement, Moonbeam wishes she could cover her mouth with masking tape. She can't believe that she is saying such things. The words just seem to spew out of her mouth uncontrollably. The conversation, however, doesn't stop there. She looks over at the man who is holding onto the table. He seems afraid.

"If you want my secrets, you must first tell me why I had to die? There was a time I trusted you. Tell me now. Who is behind this? "Moonbeam then collapses as if being let go and falls to the ground. She blurts out, "Could I have been channeling Jocko?"

She quickly remembers why and crawls back away from the man.

"Please sir, those are not my words but the Captain's. You must understand that."

The man nods "Yes'. He continues, "Tell your captain his answer is Humberto."

Moonbeam now has a new name to give Mariah and Bill.

"Humberto?" she repeats.

"I don't know if I can regain communications with him. Please wait."

Moonbeam gets up from the floor and sits down next to her customer again. She closes her eyes and raises her arms almost fearful of what she may find.

"Oh spirits please return the Captain to me. I have his answer." Moonbeam's body jerks back. She no longer has control of her movements. In a deep voice she says, "I am here. I have heard. Here is your clue.

In a box very sound
Much gold and green can be found
Resting deep in the center of the land
Where it shall not be taken by any pirate's hand."

The voice then lets out a loud laugh, "Ho ho ho Good luck my fat little traitor. Here's hoping you don't succeed, but take my advice. Watch out for the serpent. He will uncover your secret and that will prove deadly"

With that, Moonbeam falls to the ground again. Exhausted, she looks up at the man. She is out of breath. She notices that his tanned skin has paled a few shades. He knows she is not faking and is just as surprised as she is.

He looks at her, takes his hat off of the table and gets up.

"Don't get up. I will show myself out. You have told me what I need to know. There is even more than I thought."

With that, he exits Moonbeam's cottage. She is still on the floor wondering what has just happened. Kira is meowing in the next room anxious to see that her mistress is all right.

CHAPTER TWENTY-EIGHT

Moonbeam manages to drag herself up slowly. She opens the bedroom door for Kira. "Did I really do that?" she wonders as she goes into her bathroom to tidy up. She looks in the mirror." I look like I've just been electrocuted." Her hair is standing up straight from their roots, her make-up smeared and her clothes disheveled.

She quickly changes, fixes her face, combs her hair and goes to the front room. The phone is ringing and ringing but Moonbeam is in a trance-like state from her last visitor and doesn't answer it. Ironically Gray Eagle is shopping nearby and drops in for a surprise visit just in time to answer the phone. He takes a message and then turns to look at Moonbeam. "What on earth just happened to you?"

"Oh Eagle, you wouldn't believe me if I told you. I had a client. He was a man, a strange little man with a Spanish accent or perhaps Mexican, who came by hoping I could connect him with the dead. He wanted to reach Jocko. Oddly enough I did. I channeled Jocko. I have never done that before. Jocko gave the man a riddle. There was a burning ascot. Oh I must reach Mariah."

"Take your time, my friend. Your true powers shouldn't surprise you. Catch your breath and call her. I will wait here."

Moonbeam takes a deep breath. She is grateful to have Gray Eagle as a friend; he believes in her.

But she has to reach Mariah.

She dials the store only to hear Shane pick up. "Seabliss Video. Open 'til 11 P.M." Shane sounds pretty chipper, but Moonbeam is in a hurry and interrupts the store greeting. "Shane, This is Moonbeam. I have to find Mariah."

"Surprise, surprise, she's not here again but you probably know that already."

" Did she say where she was going? It's really important."

"Hey Moonie, No she didn't. All I know is that I am dog sitting Spike and she said something about going to see Bill."

Moonbeam breathes deeply, "Thanks Shane. I'll try her over there."

Mariah arrives at the police station just as Moonbeam is dialing the number.

Mariah opens the door. Bill is holding the receiver. "It's for you. Is this your new office or are all of your friends psychic?"

Mariah grabs the phone from Bill. "You are not funny."

Mariah puts the phone to her ear. She hears deep breathing on the other end and then a frantic voice.

"Mariah, it's Moonbeam. The man the man I saw in my dream came to my house. He wanted a reading on Jocko. He had his ascot. He had his ascot that means he searched his apartment…'

Mariah is shocked. "Hey slow it up. What man? What dream? You're hard to follow."

Moonbeam answers her quickly, "Sorry. The man was a short dark man rather stocky. He spoke with a Spanish accent. He said he would pay me to do a reading on Jocko because he had questions."

"Questions?" Mariah asks, "How on earth can you get Jocko to answer questions. He's dead. Remember?"

Bill gives Mariah a funny look and makes his finger circle the air near his ear expressing his feeling that Moonbeam may not have enough sandwiches to fill her picnic basket.

"Yes, yes I remember. That's what's so important. I told him he needed to pay me two hundred dollars and I would ask Jocko."

"And he paid you that much?"

"Yes. Yes so I took the ascot and held it in the air. It caught on fire like spontaneous combustion. Next thing I knew I answered questions in a voice I didn't know I had. I'm not making this up. I'm scared out of my mind. Do you suppose I did tap into the great beyond'?"

"Calm down. There has to be a rational explanation. What did this strange voice say?" Mariah is curious.

"The voice implied that there is more wealth in Jocko's fortune, mentioned someone named Humberto and told this man to beware of some serpent. Can I come over? I don't want to be alone. A killer…a serpent…the whole thing blows my mind."

Mariah sighs, "Sure come on over. Bill's here as well. Maybe he can make sense out of this." Moonbeam hangs up the phone and heads for the police station as quickly as her legs would go.

CHAPTER TWENTY-NINE

Just before Moonbeam's anticipated arrival, Mariah wants to brief Bill on Moonbeam's newest discovery.

"OK, Bill. Moonbeam called. She said she had just channeled Jocko for an unusual client."

"Aren't they all?" Bill interrupts.

"Bill, will you listen? A new name is now in the mix. Humberto whoever that is. She's coming right over to explain."

"Thanks for the warning." Bill opens his desk drawer and pulls out some alien antennas he uses on Halloween to make the local kids laugh. "Do I look ready?" he chuckles.

Moonbeam walks briskly but with a heavy heart. It is as if she knows that whatever she will feel the next time she holds the cane will be soaked with a ghostly presence. She turns down the side street and then makes her way to the front door of the station. She reaches out and opens the large screen door. "Mariah, please tell me that you're still here?"

Moonbeam does not wait for a response, she throws open the front door. She is breathing hard and looks quite pale. She starts to speak as if in the middle of a conversation.

"I swear it wasn't a trick. I never had this happen before. I must have my grandmother's gift."

Bill puts his feet up on the desk and leans back in his swivel chair. His antennae are bobbing.

"OK, Moonie, tell us about new news only."

Moonbeam takes a deep breath She sits down on a chair near the desk.

"Bill I was in the middle of a strange dream when one of the men from the dream appears at my front door. He is real. Any rate he pays me two hundred dollars to find out more about Jocko's treasure or the one he believes that Jocko has."

"Two hundred dollars? Boy am I in the wrong job," Bill interjects.

"Hold on let me finish. He had Jocko's ascot. He must have gone to the apartment after you both left. I held the ascot and the man's hat in the air and summoned the spirits. I did not really expect to reach anyone but suddenly the ascot started to burn and I'm talking like Jocko. The man said that Jocko died because of Humberto and Jocko told him that the rest of his treasure is in a box in the land. That's it in a nut shell."

"Yeah, nut shell is the right term." is Bill's only response a bit afraid of asking too many questions for fear of hearing about too much magic.

"Did you get the man's name?" Mariah chimes in hoping to carry the ball forward.

"No I was too afraid. In my dream, he was going to kill me." Moonbeam answers.

"Would you recognize him again if you saw him? Can you describe him to me?" Bill likes where this conversation is going.

"Yes, Bill. Yes, Bill I would recognize him. He was short, stocky, well tanned complexion. He was older maybe in his sixties and spoke with an accent. " Moonbeam responds proudly. "I took his curse away from the two of you. He is pure evil through and through. I can feel it."

Mariah is quiet. She paces around the small office obviously deep in thought.

"Moonie, did he say where he was staying?"

"No and I didn't want to know," Moonbeam answers honestly to her friend. "Oh I almost forgot, Jocko warned him about a serpent. A killer serpent and to beware of it"

"I guess there are a lot of people for us to beware of," Bill interjects, "And this serpent's venom is just for the mystery man."

"Yes," Moonbeam answers, "But we should watch out for all the rest."

"Well let's see, there's quite a few. Taggert hated Jocko because Bella still has feelings for the Captain and, oh yes, he was a rival captain. Oh and there's Bella, seems she was dumped for a younger woman just when the old Captain came into some cash. Maybe even Anna…Who knows why? Maybe he got too old for her and what about that little pudgy guy who came in to tell us about the final arrangements.

Let's not leave out Alejandro. Who knows? There may be friends we haven't met yet."

Mariah remains quiet. The person she doesn't know about is the one that concerns her the most. Maybe someone threatened Jocko knowing how much money he had tied up in emeralds. Maybe like the pirates that roamed these waters in the past, Jocko had other hidden booty. Mariah is amazed at how little she actually knew about her friend and yet how much she trusted him. Mariah's mind drifts back to a day when Moonbeam warned her that someone she cared about would be in grave danger. That person was Jocko and her warning came after one of their secret readings. Oh, if she only took Moonbeam's warning more seriously.

CHAPTER THIRTY
OJUANA, MEXICO

Word of Jocko's untimely death spreads quickly to this tiny Mexican village. Jocko's caring ways touched so many of its residents; his death puts this entire village in mourning. His passing is part of every conversation as the town becomes draped in a deep sadness. Black ribbons and wreaths of white flowers hang on the factory's front door as well as on the entrance to the church.

Jocko was beloved for his kindness and generosity; for most villagers, his passing is like losing a concerned and caring king. They remember with pride how Jocko cared enough about Ojuana to pay for a playground at the church.

The workers in the pottery factory are personally saddened by Jocko's death. He was a not just a good employer but a very good friend to all of them. Jose, who does the glazing, recounts tearfully, "I didn't have a car to take my youngest daughter to the doctor in the next town. She had a very high fever. Captain Jocko happened to be in town. He drove me and the baby there, paid for the doctor, and did not dock my pay. I will miss him." So will all of the workers because the Captain paid them well and cared about how their families lived.

Their alternative employer, Luis, scares them to death. His own men are afraid of him. Jocko's workers sense that Luis might threaten Anna again with violence. They fear greatly for her safety as well as their own.

Ojuana and Seabliss share the common markers of small town life. When a memorable event such as the death of a beloved resident occurs, everyone in town learns about it quickly through the many chains of local gossip. In Ojuana, many seem to know that Anna went to Seabliss before Jocko's death as did Pacco. They have also learned of Luis' departure and are puzzled. Where did he go? How does he know about Jocko? Rumors are spinning like a child's top in a playroom.

Word soon comes back from Anna that Jocko is to be cremated. She phones her foreman, "Juan, you know about Jocko's death." Anna is trying to hold back tears but can't. "I need your help in making his final arrangements. I need you and the men to create the most beautiful cremation urns possible. They must have two dolphins swimming in a circle at their widest part. The urns need special attention that I will tell you about now." Juan has been making funeral urns for many years but listens carefully to Anna's unique instructions.

Juan instructs his men, "We have to do our best work for the Captain. The instructions came directly from Anna herself. I have to insist that you follow them explicitly or we may upset her." They all understand this; unfortunately that's all they can do for Jocko now.

The urns to be cast are very large and ornate. They design the intertwining dolphins to be used in the center. The unusual oversized urns will have large classic bases. The men work magic with the clay. After all, they are working for a man they loved. The women do the same with their colorful paint and glaze until the two magnificent urns are perfect. The factory workers are proud of their memorial. Now that their work is complete, they all breathe a sigh of relief knowing that they did not let Anna or Jocko down.

The urns once finished are packed with the utmost care in large crates in preparation for the journey to Florida. The crates are to be loaded on some of the larger fishing boats going to the area. The local captains can always use the extra money. The large crates are split up between two boats heading for the Florida coast. Once there, they will be delivered to the mortuary in Seabliss. There is much sadness surrounding this particular job. Many of the women who watch cry as they remember how kind the old Captain was to them. Many of the sturdy men trying to be stoic wipe their eyes. They cry not only for the Captain but also for themselves. They all fear that the days of peace and prosperity may be gone forever for all of them.

CHAPTER THIRTY-ONE

At the exact time that the funeral urns are being trucked to the docks in Ojuana, Moonbeam and Mariah are leaving the police station. They walk slowly toward the main street and stop. Mariah wants to be out of Bill's hearing range.

"Moonie, don't look so glum. Jocko would be proud of you."

"Oh, Mariah you really think so."

"I'm not psychic but I know so. Now let's get down to business. I think we should pay a visit to our three new friends."

Did you hear what you said, three."

"Moonie, curb it. Your necklace was just a coincidence. We need to head to the Twin Palm Inn and The Blue Heron Inn. Maybe we can find answers to the too many of the questions surrounding Jocko's death. Maybe you'll get another feeling. Maybe we'll see who they really are. We can do this. Ready?"

"Ready."

The two return to the station and get in Mariah's Mustang convertible. They drive a short distance and then park around the corner, midway to both Inns in an effort not to be noticed. The best way to keep their visit clandestine is to keep that easily recognized car out of sight. Everyone in town knows who owns it.

Mariah and Moonbeam then quickly discuss how to go undercover, a task that should prove extremely difficult for each of them since both are so well known on the island. Going undercover for Mariah is almost impossible unless of course it's Halloween. Moonbeam will have just as much trouble. Her unusual dress and mannerisms make her stick out like a sore thumb. The two women get out of the car.

Mariah thoughtfully begins, "Moonbeam, we have to split up so that so that no-one will connect us being here together. I'll visit the Twin Palm. Maybe you could go down the street to the Blue Heron where Anna is staying. It's only two blocks from here. Walk around the grounds. See if you find her room. See if Anna looks despondent or elated at the thought of spending a great deal of money. I know that you only saw her through her black veil so I brought something to help you. Here's a photo I swiped from Jocko's file."

Moonbeam gasps at the thought of stealing evidence. "Shhh... We're just borrowing it. I couldn't tell Bill. He'd have a fit!" Mariah assures Moonbeam.

Moonbeam takes the long silk flowered scarf from her shoulders and places it over her head. "OK Mariah, I'm ready!" She looks at the photo carefully and then puts it in her purse. She turns abruptly and starts to walk briskly toward The Blue Heron.

Mariah watches Moonbeam walk off. "Whew, I'm glad she's going there because Anna will not be as suspicious of her as she would be of me. She'll think Moonie is there to do a reading. Maybe Moonie can get close enough to her to hone in on her feelings or overhear a conversation that may relate to Jocko."

The Blue Heron is by far one of the prettiest B&B's on the island. It is located directly on the bay. The Inn is painted a vibrant tanzanite blue with a crisp white trim. The building is a U shaped structure giving all of the rooms a view of the water. It is two stories high and has a kidney shaped pool surrounded by white bougainvillea and peach colored hibiscus. On the property are six individual cottages lined up on the water next to the main part of the inn. Each room has a sitting area, kitchenette and a small porch with white wicker rockers. The Blue Heron is the perfect setting for total rest and relaxation.

Moonbeam, however, is not looking to relax. She's on the hunt for a killer. She's a fast walker so she reaches the inn rather quickly. She knows where the office is as she has come here many times to do readings for guests.

Familiar with the lay of the land, Moonbeam first goes to the pool to take a look at the tourists sitting there. She studies the photo of Anna before her investigative perusal of the grounds looking carefully at each of the faces as she goes by. She sighs to herself, "No luck here. That might've been too easy."

She then continues up the white brick path until she reaches the main building. Smiling, she nods to guests as they pass studying each of their faces hoping to see one that looks like Anna's, but again no luck.

Moonbeam knows that having psychic powers are nice but as a back up there's nothing better than modern technology. She truly enjoys visiting those tacky spy stores in the mall. After watching one of their demonstrations, she couldn't help herself. She broke down and bought a mini spy camera. It actually comes in handy in her business helping her keep tabs on her regulars for future reference. She knows that her mini camera may be worth its weight in greenbacks right now.

Not one person, absolutely no one not even Doc or Mariah knows anything about this camera. Well, maybe Gray Eagle knows but he doesn't count; he works with her. Moonbeam opens her bag part way to check the film. "Yep," she thinks, "I still have about a dozen shots left. That may be all I need. I just have to find Anna."

Moonbeam is heading toward the Blue Heron's dock. The old dock is so long, it appears as if could dissolve into the bay. It stretches way out into the water in the same manner that the grand docks of the 30's and 40's did waiting for ferries from the mainland filled with tourists and island residents.

Moonbeam walks by guests conversing on the dock's benches. She looks into their faces but none of them are Anna. It's noon and hot; Moonbeam is getting a bit thirsty. She pulls a small flask filled with water from her purse and gulps some down. Once refreshed, she continues to walk behind the cottages where she hears some women talking. No luck, none of them have foreign accents.

Moonbeam wonders if Anna could have opted for plastic surgery in such a short time or if she's able to transform herself into another form of matter. Moonbeam's vivid imagination soon stops its possibilities; she now has to resort to the front desk.

Moonbeam can be quite the con when necessary and mentions to the young clerk that she is looking for the lady in the photograph. The clerk asks "Why?" Quick on her feet, Moonbeam responds, "She left one of her expensive earrings at my cottage yesterday after a reading. I can tell that it's expensive and I would like to return it."

The clerk has seen Moonbeam before and thinks it a nice gesture. "Well Miss Moonbeam, that's really very nice of you. That lady is in cabin four. She asked for privacy, however, and stays pretty much to herself except for this one man who keeps coming around. He has been here almost every day since she arrived. I'm guessing he must be her boyfriend." Living on a small island for any length of time makes resort workers interest in tourists' activities a hobby of sorts.

Moonbeam is surprised to hear about Anna's visitor. "Cabin four, thank you very much for your help." She then hands the clerk a dollar bill and a card for a free reading. She quickly turns and leaves.

As Moonbeam heads for Cabin four, Mariah has already returned to her car. She searched the grounds of the Twin Palm Inn but couldn't find hide or hair of Alejandro. She begins to believe that Alejandro is either a ghost or an illusionist who can make himself invisible upon demand.

"I hope Moonbeam is getting somewhere." Mariah thinks. "I will definitely hear from Bill about my borrowing that photo of Anna."

As Mariah waits, Moonbeam is hoping to work some of her magic. She walks to cabin four pulling her scarf over her face. She approaches the cabin slowly and reaches in her purse for the camera.

Moonbeam has spent so much time at The Blue Heron doing private readings that she knows the order of cabins pretty well. She walks through the courtyard straight to Anna's. As she approaches the unit, she sees that the blinds are closed but not tight enough; someone could get a peak inside between the cracks.

Moonbeam walks cautiously toward the window sideways so as not to create a large shadow. She peeks in carefully and is able to see two shadowy figures. A tall man and woman embrace. Moonbeam takes out her spy camera and uses the extra strength zoom to get a better look through the cracks in the blinds. There she is. Moonbeam recognizes Anna. Lo and behold, Anna and Alejandro are in the midst of a passionate embrace as if they are two long lost lovers finding themselves once again. Moonbeam takes as many photos as her camera will allow. "I really don't think they'll even notice me given their present state of mind."

"Mariah should be more than pleased, "Moonbeam thinks as she walks away from cabin four clutching some very valuable information in her hands.

CHAPTER THIRTY-TWO

Bill is back at the station seated at his desk. He squirms around on his seat feeling very anxious. His male intuition tells him that he shouldn't have left the two friends alone. His mind keeps going over the clues that have been collected so far. He decides to review his evidence box. Looking through it, he notices that Anna's photo is missing. "What? Who would have done a sneaky underhanded thing like that? Miss Mariah, perhaps? Wait until I see her. She could get me fired." Bill's face turns beet red.

He leans back in his large brown office chair hoping that the phone will ring. It's hard for him to be so idle when there is so much to investigate surrounding Jocko's untimely death. Right now, Bill wouldn't mind any kind of call even if it's only to accompany the paramedics to a stingray bite. As he reads the newest issue of "Popular Handguns," he hears the sound of a car pulling up. By the sound of the motor, he knows that it's not just any car, it's Mariah's. He's relieved she's back so she can return the photo. "The chief would have my head if he ever found out."

Bill's mind continues, "I wonder where they those two dizzy dames went? I wonder if they are getting into more trouble trying to find new evidence?"

The front door to the station opens quickly. Mariah and Moonbeam enter all smiles. Mariah clears her throat as if to designate a great announcement. She begins, "Well, Bill, won't you be surprised. We have something that will actually help with the investigation."

Bill sits back in his desk chair with his arms crossed waiting for some nonsense to come out of the two women's mouths. But surprisingly enough, they do not speak. Instead Moonbeam pulls out an envelope containing photos from her purse. Moonbeam hands the package to Bill, "Bill, I took them with my mini spy camera. That's what took us so long; I had to develop them in my little dark room at work."

"Mini spy camera, dark room, Moonie what on earth do you need those for?" Bill looks up almost laughing.

"Don't ask and I won't tell. Besides, Gray Eagle uses it as much as I do.

It's become a hobby for him," Moonbeam looks a bit ruffled at her own admission as she hands the envelope over to Bill. Bill begins to look at the photos. "Well, Lookee here, kids," he says slowly, "The grieving widow is not so grieving. This sure changes the look of the landscape. Speaking of photos, I want the one of Anna that you took!"

Mariah silently digs in her purse to pull out the photo of Anna. She hands it to Bill who gives her a look. He quickly returns it to the evidence file.

"Mariah, you could've got me fired! How could you?"

Mariah just stares at the floor.

"OK never mind, has anyone visited the mortuary to see who has claimed Jocko's remains and where they plan to lay him to rest?"

Mariah pauses, "No Bill I guess I was so upset that I didn't want to interfere with a private matter in case Jocko really did have family. Now I realize we should. Who knows what these people are planning."

"Right" Bill answers quickly," So, let's go there right now." Bill radios for Johnson to come back. "Get in here and hold down the fort?"

"Sure, Chief, no problem," Johnson responds anxious to get his hands on Bill's magazines and take a break.

As soon as the deputy arrives, the three leave the small station in a hurry and pile into Bill's unmarked jeep so as not to draw attention to a police matter. Bill asks, "OK Everybody in? We're going to the funeral home to see who's claiming Jocko's remains." With that, Bill backs out of the narrow driveway.

During the short drive to the Shell Mortuary, Bill wants to establish some ground rules for the two women to approach the mortician, Mr. Grimley. Bill speaks as if he is thinking out loud,

"Mariah, maybe you and Moonie should go visit old Mr. Grimley without me. We don't want to make this look like an official police visit. I doubt if Grimley is involved in anyway but just in case we don't want to tip our hand. We have a better chance of getting any information out of him if you two very saddened friends express your concern. I'll park the jeep down the street and out of sight. Once inside, see what you can see and ask as many questions with deference of course, as you can. Capish?"

Both women nod affirmatively.

Moonbeam smiles. "I feel that great things will begin with this visit. Jocko will be pleased."

Bill drives down a narrow island dirt road and parks the jeep a block south of the mortuary.

CHAPTER THIRTY-THREE
THAT SAME AFTERNOON

The tall handsome man holds Anna close to him. He kisses her forehead."
Our wait will be over soon. Stay strong." With that, he leaves.

Anna, however, is very anxious. Soon after his departure, she decides to
leave the inn to check on any special delivery packages to her from Ojuana.
Anna instructed the factory to ship the urns to the little office supply store on
the island not too far from her hotel. The store often accepts, with proper prior
arrangements, deliveries for visitors for a small fee.

When Anna enters the store, her exotic Latin looks instantly turn heads.
The young clerk, Dave, is quickly smitten. "Hello young man, I am waiting for
some special delivery packages from Mexico. My name is Anna. Have they
arrived?"

Dave, the master of procrastination, can make customers actually believe
that he is working when stalling is his middle name.

"Ma'am, if you can wait just one minute, I'll be more than happy to go in
the back room and check." He's in the storage room a good ten minutes making
Anna start to pace. She notices that after all of that time, old Dave comes out
empty handed. As he informs Anna that her packages have not arrived yet, she
becomes furious. She utters some nasty words in Spanish, a language that
Dave understands fluently and then leaves the store quickly heading straight
for a payphone where she believes that her call cannot be traced. Anna calls
her factory.

"Good Morning," a familiar worker's voice answers, "Pots by Anna."

"Marco," Anna asks, "Did you ship the urns for Jocko. Did they go out?
When? And how I ask of you?"

"Si, Senora, they were shipped as asked. Why? What is wrong? They have
not arrived yet?"

"I am truly sorry, Senora Anna, I shipped them as directed. You know that sometimes customs interferes. Maybe they got detained in customs."

That is not exactly the kind of news that Anna wants to hear. "Ok Marco, I'll see if Pacco has picked them up from one of the safe entries."

Anna hangs up the phone and returns to the office supply store to see what she can find out about that shipment.

Dave, now fully aware of her temper, makes a few calls to hopefully dilute her constant questions. Unfortunately, there's no news. Dave has to lie or face her temper again. He hesitates for a minute and then sheepishly begins, "M'am, I traced your shipment back to arriving in Florida sometime last week. The customs station where they entered the country is evidently backlogged big time. They could be sitting in a warehouse with hundreds of other boxes awaiting clearance. Lately, we have seen many late shipments and delays just because of that. I know that this is not what you want to hear but some people have had to wait as long as two or three extra weeks."

With that news, Anna is biting her lip so hard it could bleed. "Two weeks? That is not acceptable. They are for a memorial service."

Anna cannot accept the fact that a clerk is just a clerk and he cannot fight the US government. She has become accustomed to better service at home. Of course, she now has the right connections. Dave has been working at the store for a long time and is used to people being upset by delays. After all, everyone needs his order yesterday. It is no wonder that the owner of the store is rarely around.

Dave looks at Anna with his rehearsed pity. "I am deeply sorry for this delay. If it will help you, I will check on your package again tomorrow"

At this point, Anna does not know what to do. Of course, she cannot go to customs; she is not supposed to be here let alone the fact that she's involved with that shipment.

She looks at Dave with a very sad look, also rehearsed, and fakes a few tears. "Oh, What ever you can do to help me bring my Captain home to his family. I will be eternally grateful."

With that, Anna dressed in a provocatively low cut black dress, turns and leaves the small store. Dave, watching her departure, is obviously taken by her beauty and because of that, his promise to call will actually materialize.

CHAPTER THIRTY-FOUR

The Shell Mortuary is one of the oldest and most respected businesses on the island. The Grimley family started it back in the early 1900's and Mr. Winston Grimley, a descendant of its founder, still runs it to this day.

The facility is located on a quiet but pretty side street. Mr. Grimley takes great pride in its appearance with well-manicured lawns and a centrally located beautiful memorial garden filled with bright colored tropical flowers and orchids as a focal point. The garden's landscaping is framed with concrete statues of sea life creating a sense of peace and serenity.

The sidewalk leading to the large mahogany front door is composed of broken shells mixed with cement to recreate an old-fashioned island walkway. "As my grandfather always told us," Mr. Grimley likes to recant, "If the outside is right, people will be confidant that our work inside will be right as well."

Bill parks under a large Australian pine tree. Since he has decided to wait for Mariah and Moonbeam in the car, he puts the radio on low so he can hear it but it will not be distracting to people walking by.

Mariah and Moonbeam get out of the car. Moonbeam looks at Bill, "OK wish us luck. We're off to see the wizard." The two walk together down the street, up the sidewalk until they reach the massive front door. They knock twice using a huge brass knocker in the shape of a shell and the door slowly opens.

Mariah and Moonbeam are surprised to see that it is Mr. Grimley himself who greets them. Grimley is an imposing figure, rather tall and pale in complexion with kind black eyes. He is always dressed in a dark suit. Mariah has never seen him any other way wondering what he wears to the beach.

Grimley takes his business seriously but not himself. On Halloween, he answers the door with a face covered in white powder, a mouth dripping of fake blood, and a black cape. He can make any vampire proud as well as scaring the little local trick or treaters silly. They love to be scared and return every year. Of course, the extra large candy bars help.

Grimley knows both ladies, as they are all part of the island's business network. "Hello, Mariah and Moonbeam. What a pleasant surprise. What brings this unexpected visit? How can I help you? Oh, my goodness, how rude of me, please do come in."

The women follow Grimley through the large wood paneled foyer laden with antiques to his equally large office. Mr. Grimley escorts them in and signals with his hand for the two women to be seated in two large leather armchairs. "Please, come, sit down. Tell me how I can be of service to you."

Mariah starts, "Mr. Grimley, we deeply appreciate your hospitality. You more than anyone on the island know how close I am or was to Captain Jocko. He is…was one of my dearest friends. I am deeply saddened by his death and am concerned that his final arrangements are properly taken care of as I am not aware of his mentioning any next of kin."

Moonbeam remains quiet but is impressed. Mariah has always been quick on her feet when needed. Moonbeam nods her head in agreement and poses a faint smile.

Mariah continues. She knows that she is on a roll. "Has his family been notified? In all the years I knew Jocko I am embarrassed to say that I don't know if he even has any relatives."

Mr. Grimley always looks serious since serious is the nature of his business. "Mariah, first of all, let me tell you how saddened I am by your loss. The whole island community will miss Captain Jocko. As far as I know, he has no family locally but someone, I am assuming a good friend, has offered to pay for the funeral arrangements and claim his remains. Give me a moment to look up that information. I know that this is not customary but I do know personally how close you were to the Captain. If I can ease your heart by telling you what I can about it, then it is my job to do so. I wish I could remember the exact details. It's tough getting old. You just don't remember every little detail like you should. That's why I keep thorough files."

Grimley gets up, goes over to the antique oak file cabinet behind his desk and opens the top drawer marked "Current Arrangements." Jocko's file is at the very front of the file. Grimley pulls it out.

"Oh yes here it is. Let's see."

Grimley slowly fumbles through all of the loose papers. "Ah yes, A person named Anna…hard to pronounce her last name…has claimed his remains.

She is also paying for all of the final arrangements. She asks that his body be cremated as quickly as possible after we receive it from the medical examiner. She says that she has two beautiful urns being made in her pottery factory in Mexico to hold his ashes. Oh yes, and the reason for the two urns is so that the ashes will be divided equally between herself and Jocko's son. Well, I guess he does have next of kin in Mexico then. Maybe his son could not afford to take care of all of this. Very kind of this beautiful lady to do so, don't you think?"

The two women sit quietly. They nod affirmatively to Grimley's comment as both think simultaneously that Grimley noticed Anna's good looks.

Grimley puts the file away. Mariah is somewhat surprised by this information as well as the fact that Grimley is so obviously taken in by Anna. However, she manages to keep her cool. Anything else would work against her goal. She clears her throat as if she is touched by Mr. Grimley's information. She finds the following question hard for her to get out. "Ahem, has Jocko been cremated yet?"

"No, Mariah, not yet." Grimley responds in a kind voice noticing how difficult the subject is for Mariah." We are waiting for the coroner to release his remains. That decision rests solely with the M.E. and of course the police department. Evidently, they are still running tests on the deceased for whatever reason. They assured me that they would call when it is appropriate."

Mariah and Moonbeam breathe a deep sigh of relief almost simultaneously but they know that they must learn more. Looking around his office at his wall of awards for community service, Mariah asks, "Will Anna have a final service for Jocko here before his remains are sent to Mexico?"

Grimley is slow to respond. He is sure that his answer will disappoint Mariah. "No, Anna has made no such plans. Her directions for us are to cremate Jocko, dispense his ashes between the two urns and prepare the urns for shipment to Mexico. A service would be a nice idea, however, Jocko did have many friends here. If you want one, maybe I could arrange for a private one after his ashes were placed in the urns. That might ease your grief and help you say goodbye properly."

Mariah's eyes swell with real tears. "Thank you Mr. Grimley. That would be most kind. I would greatly appreciate that."

Moonbeam silently nods in agreement again. She knows that she has been silent for the entire visit but feels that she is more helpful if she looks like she is there for moral support. The women rise slowly from their seats, shake hands with Mr. Grimley and leave. Moonbeam holds Grimley's hand a little longer than Mariah.

Both silent; both deep in thought, they walk slowly around the block to Bill. Mariah looks up at Bill and is suddenly brought back into reality.

"What a mess!" She exclaims as she sees shredded lettuce, onions and bread crust all over the police department's unmarked jeep. It seems Bill got bored waiting so he went back to Mariah's store and picked up Spike. They went for a ride and ended up at the local sub shop. Bill got a roast beef sub to go and they split it.

Spike is still enjoying his half in the backseat shaking the shredded lettuce out of the sandwich first.

"Don't you have any police business to do, Bill. I know you are on a stakeout but that's spelled s-t-a-k-e and not s-t-e-a-k. Is that all you can do? Eat, wait, and mess up the jeep."

"Yes M'am, you got that right," Bill smiles, "I hear that a lot, mostly jokes about donuts. Now what have you two amateur detectives found out?"

"Well, for starters," Mariah begins," Anna is paying for the funeral. She wants Jocko cremated as quickly as possible. His ashes are then to be divided and placed in two urns one for Anna and the other for Jocko's son, But Jocko has no son. I know that."

Bill is quiet for a minute and then asks, "Are you sure? Are you really really sure? After all you did not know about this Anna until she actually showed up? A mistake like that could make the police look very foolish."

Mariah folds her arms defiantly, "Yes I'm sure. Very sure."

"So why are his ashes being divided up? And where are they going?" Bill asks out loud.

Mariah remains defiant, "To Anna and Alejandro. Something's up and it's something big. Something that probably involves those emeralds."

Bill sits up trying to absorb all of this new information. He looks at Mariah and Moonbeam, "OK girls hop in with the Shredder and we'll all go back to the office where we can try to piece this out."

Moonbeam is smart; she gets in the front seat with Bill.

"Oh Spike," Mariah blurts out, "I'm sitting in lettuce."

As usual, Spike just wags his tail. He loves the sound of Mariah's voice and starts kissing her. Bill turns the key, "All set, ladies. We'll go back and try to uncover the truth about this whole mess. I'll bet whoever's involved in the murder may just be involved in Jocko's funeral plans."

Ying and Yang. As Bill and crew make their way back to the beach station parking lot, the two fishing boats carrying those special urns are making their way across the Gulf of Mexico and onto the Florida coastline. The loyal factory workers did just as they were told; now they hope that their local fishermen will get the merchandise through customs undamaged at one of the more rural customs stations.

Many who deal in transporting cargo for years believe that the choice of a customs stations is based on luck. Actually luck has nothing to do with it, as any successful smuggler well knows. Researching an area to find the most remote, the most understaffed, and overworked customs station is just as important as luck. When customs agents are too busy, a package easily slips through the watchful eyes of local officials. Luis, for one, has been smuggling for a long time and has learned that a good strategy is the key. After all, he is the master.

The station that Anna instructed the factory to use is isolated and small. Located at the beginning of the Everglades, it has been very understaffed. Once the crates are in and through customs, the urns will be trucked across the state. Unbeknownst to her, however, this station has just had a recent staff change. Longtime customs officer Snake Ringster, a one-man force and likes it that way, has moved there from Miami and is now in charge.

CHAPTER THIRTY-FIVE

When the peculiar trio of investigators reaches the station, Bill sees that the envelope containing the toxicology report is still on his desk. As he opens it again, he sits down. Mariah and Moonbeam anxiously watch hoping that he sees something he didn't see before.

"I'll be damned." Bill begins, "I keep reading this but the report looks clean except for the digitoxin. Jocko was administered a heavy dose of digitoxin. The drug when taken in excess recreates the symptoms of a heart attack since the reaction is immediate, it could've gone undetected. That's why our pretty Miss Anna wants Jocko cremated so fast hoping that we haven't found anything because we weren't smart enough to look. But why the big rush to get him to Mexico? She's definitely a prime suspect. We have to find those urns before they reach Grimley's mortuary. I'm not a gambling man but, like you said Mariah, I'll bet Jocko's ashes won't be in them alone."

Mariah begins to twist her favored curl almost to the point of knotting it. She asks questions that almost seem rhetorical. "We all know that Anna must have had something to do with it...maybe Alejandro if that's his real name as well. And what about that strange little man Pacco? But how can we prove it? Who will benefit the most from Jocko's death? How can we catch them?"

Bill looks at her sympathetically, "If we knew that, honey, we'd have this case locked up."

Moonbeam tries to help, "I know from the cosmos that Alejandro is evil through and through but unfortunately that alone is not enough to arrest him."

Bill is quiet for a moment. "I suppose I could make some calls. Ojuana is not exactly a metropolis. A shipment like that might just stand out in someone's memory."

Mariah is deep in thought not paying one bit of attention to Bill. "We know that Anna's a liar especially about Jocko's son getting half of his remains. He had no son." She says slowly.

"Mariah, you better be sure. Sure enough to bet the farm?" Bill pounces on her thoughts like a cat on a mouse." After all," he reminds her, "You have been wrong about many other things."

"I'm positive." Mariah is defiant. "Jocko told me that he did have an illegitimate child, a daughter whom he has never met. He knew that at one time she lived somewhere in California. So why is Alexandro getting that second urn?"

Bill is very quiet. "Probably for smuggling! That's why. They want to smuggle something in or out of Ojuana. We need to think like Alejandro for a few minutes. He does seem like a sharp guy in the brains department. If I were going to smuggle anything in and out of there, first thing I would do is look for the most remote US customs station I could find."

Mariah looks at him like he just hit the jackpot. "That's it, but where would he go?"

Bill sits back in his chair and smiles a long and thoughtful smile. "If he has not been to areas southeast of here recently, just by looking at the map, he might think that he would have an easier time getting his stuff in and out of Key Isle. Ha! Key Isle now has my buddy Snake on duty. Like I said before, I'm not a betting man but I would bet on Snake any day."

Moonbeam laughs, "I guess by his name alone, I might bet on Snake too." She pauses for a second, "Actually, he may be the serpent in Jocko's warning. Are you going to call him? May I listen to his voice? His voice will tell me what I need to know."

"Yes, I am going to give him a holler and it wouldn't hurt if you listened in," Bill responds.

Moonbeam, still curious, does not let up with her questions, " Why is he called Snake? Is he sneaky or does he just enjoy beating up on snakes, human or reptilian?"

Bill looks her straight in the eyes and seriously says, "It's a little bit of both, my dear."

CHAPTER THIRTY-SIX
SNAKE THE CHARMER

Snake Ringster is not just any ordinary customs officer; he is the best damn customs officer in the port of Miami. His arrest and confiscation record is so excellent that his superior officers transferred him hoping that he could straighten out all the problems at the smallest and most isolated entry port in the Keys, Key Isle. Until Snake's transfer, Key Isle had been notorious as easy access to drug dealers and smugglers. Key Isle was like an open bar to a drug smuggler; anything goes. Not now, however, there's a new bartender in town who's checking IDs!

Key Isle needs Snake's cunning ways; it is far from high tech. The main station building looks like a big cottage. It is electrically wired to the gills but with an antiquated alarm system hoping to stave off any after hour intruders.

Snake in just his brief tenure there has managed to fill the station up with some pretty valuable merchandise in which smugglers tried to use to hide illegal substances. That's exactly how Stanley Ringster earned his nickname "Snake"; he has single handedly caught more "snakes" or drug dealers than any other agent in South Florida.

Since Key Isle is the only station for miles, Snake has to cover a lot of ground. Sure one or two are able to make it through the mangroves, but on the whole, Snake takes pride in his ability to outsmart the most sophisticated adversaries.

Snake may come off as an old country bumpkin, but surprise, surprise, Snake has one of the keenest minds on the force. Having a phone and a walkie-talkie that connect him with his main headquarters in Miami, multiple guns, and pistols doesn't hurt his success rate either. Then there is his secret weapon, a big old dog, his best friend and roommate, Joe the German Shepherd. Joe is not just any old dog. He is government trained. His nose has been certified making him an official drug sniffer dog. Joe can out sniff the best of them!

At any rate, Snake and Joe share a small room at the Key Isle station. They can actually see or in Joe's case hear the boats approaching the mangroves not far from their station even under the cover of darkness. Snake and Joe know how to wait, be quiet and then go get'em.

Bill and Snake are friends who go back a long way. They met on a police case where the jurisdiction was split between the town and the federal government. The case involved a homicide committed by an illegal alien suspected of drug smuggling. That's where Snake, known as Stanley back then, came in. There wasn't enough evidence for Bill to hold the suspect for murder, but Snake could sure nail him for drugs!

Stan or Snake and Bill have always worked well together. They respect each other's experience and have a similar sense of humor. After all, they are both local boys. Both men try to stay in touch. That's a pretty hard thing to do considering the amount of hours they work. Each one does know that if the other calls for a favor, it is as good as done.

And that's exactly what Bill has in mind. As Bill dials the number for the Key Isle station, Moonbeam is sitting at another desk with her eyes closed. With one hand she holds the receiver.

With the other, she clutches her grandmother's locket, anxious to hear Snake's voice.

Just as Bill's call is making its way through the telephone wires, Snake is looking out the barred windows. He picks up his binoculars and sees two fishing vessels a bit larger than the usual ones pulling into the nearby cove. "OK Joe," Snake snaps, "Looks like we have company. Ready to go to work?" Joe wags his tail, looks out the window and utters a low growl. That growl signals to Snake that Joe is definitely ready.

Snake gets up from his chair and starts to head for the door. He is just about to turn the knob when he hears the phone ring. He runs back to his desk and picks up. "Key Isles Customs," he answers. Snake hears an all too familiar voice on the other end. "Hey Snake, What's up dude?"

Snake shakes his head and smiles, "Hey Bill is that you? Long time no see man. Long time."

Bill glances over at Moonbeam and agrees, "Yeah it's been too long. It seems that I only call when I'm working on something. We all get so busy. It's hard. I know you think I live in Paradise but we are really understaffed."

"Ditto here, man," Snake being the only agent on duty, "How can I help?"

Just as Snake says the word "help," Moonbeam feels a slight chill. It's the same chill she felt outside of Jocko's apartment right after his death. She believes that it's Jocko trying to tell her something. She carefully puts the phone receiver down. She senses that the hand holding onto the locket feels so cool and soothing at the sound of Snake's voice. She looks over at Bill and signals her approval of Snake.

"Well, Snake," Bill continues, "I'm actually loading up my jeep preparing to head your way. I need to locate two large urns that are being shipped from Mexico. I have a strong feeling that they may show up at your station. I'm betting that those guys are doing some smuggling outbound and think that Key Isle is still an easy port of entry for their plan, but now that you're there, we both know better."

"Amen man" Snake agrees.

Bill goes on, "At any rate, I'm pretty sure that one of the shippers is a noted drug dealer. I need you to hold the packages at the station as long as possible. Try to keep them in custody until I get there. Make up something. Just stall their release. I need you to do that as a favor for me. The men involved may have murdered a good friend of mine."

Snake is silent. He clears his throat and says, "For you, consider it as good as done. Can I ask who they are and where they're from?"

Bill explains, "They're from Ojuana, Mexico. I'm not sure of the dealer's real name. The urns are unusually tall and may have something to do with the murder case. If they are released to the mortuary, loaded with the victim's ashes, and sent back to Ojuana, Mexico, I guess you could say that my case goes up in smoke as well."

Snake chuckles at Bill's choice of phrasing. He repeats his promise, "I'm here for you, man. Looks like I got a couple of banditos heading in now with some cargo. Joe and I were just going out to meet them. When do you think you'll get here?"

Bill responds quickly, "I'm leaving now, so I figure four to five hours. I'll have two ladies with me. They're friends of the victim's and are helping me with the case as special deputies. Whatever you say to me, you can say to them with clean language of course."

Snake laughs, "You know me, I'm always the perfect gentleman with the ladies."

As Snake hangs up, he can see that those two boats are pulling up trying to hide in the mangroves near his station. He looks at his dog. "OK Joe let's go get'em."

Joe is not a dog to be taken lightly. He is a trained police dog who, according to Snake, got in a tug of war with a big gator trying to save a neighbor's cat. Joe won. The alligator lost and swam off. The cat, however, needed surgery on his amputated tail but thanks to Joe is fine now. "Go get'em" is the signal Joe needs to lead the tall lanky customs officer into any situation.

Snake puts down his binoculars and gets his pistol and badge. He opens the door, fastens Joe's leash and the two of them walk down the wooded path to the mangroves where the boats are docked. He can tell that they are fishermen and probably have come from Mexico. The two men may not speak English.

"Hola" Snake yells as Joe sits at attention by his side. "Hola" he repeats holding up his badge. The fishermen do not know what to do so they hold their hands in the air as if Snake is the local policia. They look scared, keeping one eye on Joe all the while.

Snake is not fluent but can talk his way through a short conversation in Spanish.

"Hola, I am not going to hurt or arrest you. Understand?"

The men put their arms down by their sides and shake their heads "yes."

"You are on United States soil. I have to check you for paper work and your boat for any shipments coming into the country. Si?"

"Si" they respond quickly.

"Do not be afraid. The dog and I must board your vessel. OK?'

The men look at each other in complete terror but they know they must do it; they respond with "OK'.

Snake and Joe walk in unison to the small boats and climb on board the first one. Snake takes off Joe's leash. "OK boy go to work." With that command, Joe sniffs out each boat. He does not appear to have found any evidence of drugs but each boat has one large container. Snake decides that he has to stall them. These may be the urns, but the fact that they appear to be drug free puzzles Snake. Neither of the men have passports which might explain why they want to hide out in the mangroves, but Snake being Snake knows there must be more to this story than meets his eyes right now.

Snake notices all of the old shredded newspapers coming out of the cracks on the sides of the containers. They obviously must contain something breakable. Each of the small boats rocks back and forth as Snake walks around the large boxes.

"OK, pal, would you please open this for me?" He motions with his hands to reinforce his request.

The fisherman nods and opens the box. Sure enough down deep amidst the paper sits one large beautiful urn. Made of clay in a natural peach color, it has dolphins swimming in all directions around the center of the urn.

Snake knows what he must try to do. He points to himself and then the box. Half in Spanish, half English, he tells the first man, "I need to hold this box overnight. I am alone here and don't have enough staff to process the necessary paperwork until tomorrow. Let me check your friend's boat and then we will bring the two boxes into the station."

Snake proceeds to the next boat and does exactly the same thing. The box is clear of drugs, but Snake wonders if this is really a diversion to cover up where the drugs might really be making entry. Snake, however, knows that he has to deal with the problem at hand

The two men and Snake then carefully unload and carry the two large boxes into the station. Joe follows close behind to make sure that neither of the fishermen is thinking of taking a detour.

Snake thanks the two men and says using as much Spanish as he can remember, "My amigos, I will try to accommodate you as quickly as I can."

The men nod as if understanding. One asks in complete sentences showing Snake that they understood the whole time, "Tomorrow maybe? What time can we come back and get them? We are responsible for them reaching trucks on shore. Someone has agreed to pick them up."

Snake thinks for a moment. "Amigos, Give me the number for the delivery person. When the merchandise has cleared customs I will call them right away personally. It should take no more than two days. You can go home now without me having to check your personal identification if you leave me that number. As I said, I work all alone except for Old Joe that is."

Not wanting to be detained as illegal, the men decide to accept Snake's offer. Snake seems to be a straight shooter and they have no identification. Since the urns are empty the men did not foresee any problems. The fishermen give Snake that all important phone number. Snake shakes their hands before they leave and thanks them for their patience. The men, happy to leave, board their boats and head for home.

Snake, on the other hand, thinks out loud. "Old Bill's hunch was right. That man either took a lucky guess or he's psychic. I know old Bill wouldn't be making the trip down to Key Isle unless I could be of even more help. What I hate is the thought that somewhere nearby, that same drug dealer who shipped those empty urns is trying to throw off the scent of his illegal shipment. I may be slow 'cause I work alone, but I'm not stupid. I have to stay focused on the urns to help Bill, but when we're done, that sneaky drug dealer is goin' to be gator bait. That I promise! Right Joe?" Joe just wags his tail.

CHAPTER THIRTY-SEVEN

While Snake is delaying the entry of the urns, Mariah, Bill and Moonbeam jump into Bill's patrol car. Spike follows but his ride is short returning him to Mariah's store. Mariah doesn't want to take Spike to Key Isle because she is afraid that Spike may run into a wayward and hungry alligator. Worse yet, she has been told that old Joe is not too fond of other dogs frequenting his station. The three make a quick stop to let Spike off, give Mariah enough time to leave instructions for the store, and then head for Key Isle.

Bill knows better than to turn on his blue flashing lights until after he crosses the main bridge to the island. He doesn't want to call attention to his road trip as well as his non-official traveling companions. One thing is sure: this trip, right or wrong, is being made for a friend.

As of now, the unusual trio of investigators are unaware of Snake's snatch; they hope that if he does find the urns, they may hold the clues needed to put the pieces of Jocko's death in order.

"Moonbeam, you'd better be right about Snake being the right guy. We're going out on a limb; no we're hanging by a limb because of your feelings. This will be a tough thing for me to explain to the chief. I hope to hell you're right. I'm going along with this because Snake hasn't been there long enough for any regular dealer to know about the change of guard. At any rate, time is of the essence, my ladies, so once we are on the main highway, hold onto your hats!" Bill says with a boyish glee as he turns those blue flashing lights on and steps on the gas.

Bill has a heavy foot normally but on this trip, his two riders really complain. "Oh Wow, We're now experiencing G-forces, Bill. Take it easy, please." Moonbeam pleads but to no avail. It takes a little over three hours to get to Snake's even with blue lights and rocket speed. The three arrive tired but alert. They soon see the long dirt road that leads to the customs house, the long wooden pier and Joe.

Bill drives slowly down the dirt road with his high beams on. The two women are yawning and trying to stretch. Bill stops the car and they all get out very slowly and stretch their legs. Bill bends over to touch his toes,

He starts to speak as if almost proud of his latest accomplishment, "What a ride!"

"I don't know about anyone else but I felt it would last forever," Moonbeam chimes in.

"Well, guess if you checked your crystal ball, Moonie, you would have known our ETA," Bill responds quickly.

Joe sees them and starts barking. His barking brings out Snake from the other side of the building. Ringster holds up his high beam flashlight and squints. When he sees who's there, he bounds across the dirt parking lot arms extended to Bill.

"Hey Dude, great to see you, even if it is because of a case. Who are your lovely traveling companions? "Snake asks with a wink.

"Snake, I'd like you to meet my temporary deputy, Mariah and her special consultant in psychology, I guess you could say, Moonbeam." Each woman raises her hand as if to say "Hi."

"Pleased to make your acquaintances, M'am's. Please everybody, come on inside and fill me in on the whole story over a cup of coffee. My coffee is known to open your eyes and keep y'all awake!"

The three follow Snake in single file to the cramped overloaded field office. Moonbeam and Mariah's eyes are wide in awe at all of the stuff Snake has managed to cram in there. Snake goes over to the coffee pot, measures the needed tablespoons of coffee, pours in some water without measuring and turns the coffee pot on. As it perks, he grabs some mugs, milk and sugar. "Some of my visitors claim that my coffee is so strong you can chew it." The pot makes a slight electric whirring noise signaling that this magic potion is ready. Snake pours out four of the strongest cups of coffee Mariah and Moonbeam have ever seen, smelled or tasted.

He hands a mug to each of them; Bill takes a big gulp right away; he's had Snake's coffee before. Mariah and Moonbeam, on the other hand, are a little more cautious. They smell the contents almost as if sniffing wine while deciding whether or not they should partake. All are seated on large shipping containers.

Snake sure seems energetic. "OK, Now that we're all comfortable. Just kidding, but these large containers are all I have for chairs. What's going on with this murder case? How can I help?"

Bill puts his mug down. "Snake, this is somewhat complicated because it involves a friend of ours who died suddenly and suspiciously. He was an old sea captain named Jocko with ties to a little village in Mexico called Ojuana on the East coast. I've found out since we spoke that this village is also home to a drug cartel with a drug lord named Luis. The locals won't tell anyone what his last name is as they are in fear of their lives. I recently received by fax a copy of a grainy photo taken by one of our FBI agents down there. It doesn't give us much to go on. Recently a man who claims to be Jocko's son and ironically resembles the FBI description of Luis has been seen in Seabliss."

Mariah and Moonbeam are surprised but impressed by Bill's homework. Bill continues," We haven't been able to pin down much evidence that links him to the crime. The only thing we do know is that the factory that Jocko owned with his secret squeeze is shipping special urns for Jocko's remains. We know that the Captain was murdered. We have reason to believe that there's a special motive behind his newly assembled family wanting to use those urns. Either they're bringing something into the US or will be shipping something out with Jocko's remains. If we know what the urns look like and figure out how they are being used, we might be able to foil their plans and trap them for smuggling or murder or both."

Snake leans forward on his crate as if to listen more intently. He is grinning ear to ear. He moves around a little on his seat but remains very quiet. Bill knows that when Snake is that quiet, the man is thinking.

"Well, Bill, I have a surprise for you. Joe and I are holding for inspection today, urns that seem to match your description. I have them in my possession as well as the contact number for the pick-up agent. I guess as an agent of the law, if you suspect foul play, then you should order me to open the containers and carefully examine what's inside."

The three from Seabliss are pleasantly surprised. "Snake you are just as wonderful as Bill said," Mariah bursts out.

"Well M'am, that's appreciated, but we only have the urns, not the culprits. Old Joe here is just as responsible for this as I am." Joe, who had come in and lay down by Snake, sits up at attention wagging his tail.

"Enough with the compliments come with me." With that, Snake gets up and starts walking to the door that leads to the adjacent overstuffed warehouse room. 'Come on y'all, let's take a look." He smiles as he leads them directly to the two large crates.

"Here they are kids," Snake starts to empty all of the shredded newspapers into another nearby empty box so that he will be able to put them back together the same way that they came when he's done. Once emptied, Snake carefully holds up each precious cargo, an exquisite pottery urn. The urns are in a natural clay color with intertwining dolphins embossed in the pottery very stately, very dignified. They are tall, wide in the mouth of the vase and wider still at the very bottom. All four stare at their shape carefully. Snake gets out his powerful flashlight." Hey Bill, hold this a minute." He looks down into one. "Well, lookee here. This is a pretty tall vase for being so shallow. Why do they need two of these, anyway?"

Bill begins to explain, "They are splitting the Captain's remains in half and shipping each half back separately."

Snake looks a bit puzzled, "Huh? Say that again. Sounds like a con job to me."

Mariah cannot help but become involved in this conversation. She walks around the urns examining them closely. "Snake, they want to split up the ashes and send one to his lover and one to a son that does not exist. Look at how tall these things are. Could we check the bottom to see if they are hollowed out and may contain something?"

"That, my pretty lady, is my next thought as well," Snake smiles. He taps the sides of the urns. "They sound as hollow as a drum. Besides, old Joe had a good whiff. There is nothing in them now." The four are silent deep in thought.

Snake breaks the silence, "Bill, do me a favor. Hold onto this urn again as I tip it sideways to examine the bottom." Snake pushes the urn toward Bill and gets down on his knees to examine the bottom. He sees what looks like a panel made of the same clay that gently pushes against the bottom. Moonbeam closes her eyes and starts to chant. Mariah looks at what Snake is doing. Using a small pocket screwdriver, Snakes slides the panel just enough to see if it is concealing something. "Lookee here, look at these four rather large compartments." Mariah and Moonbeam get down on the floor to see what Snake sees. They look at each other realizing that they may be getting close.

Snake looks at Bill, "These urns are definitely designed by professional smugglers. Whatever they want to bring into Ojuana besides Jocko's ashes will fit nicely on the bottom of these puppies. The contact person from the delivery service may actually lead us to the real smuggling operation."

"Whatever you need us to do, Snake, we're there, Bill affirms.

Snake and Bill carefully hold the urns upright. They are somewhat heavy but more awkward. Working together gives them a little insurance that they won't drop and break them. They lift the urns and place them in their original containers and return the packing inside each crate.

Snake looks at the three tired but eager assistants, "Why don't the three of you wait here. I want to make a phone call in private. What did you say the name of the mortuary is?"

Bill interjects, "I didn't."

Mariah looks at Bill wondering if Snake is trustworthy. Bill reads her mind and gives her a reassuring look. He smiles as if he knows what Snake is thinking. "I didn't say, Snake, but it's called The Shell Mortuary.'

"How appropriate," Snake retorts.

"Snake I have the number in my notebook." Bill takes his pocket notebook out and grabs a piece of scrap paper and a pencil off of one of the boxes. "Here it is."

"Thanks," Snake smiles. "Make yourselves comfortable kids. Anybody want more coffee?"

All three shake their heads "no."

"OK, then, I'll be back in a jiff."

With that Snake closes the door to his cramped office and leaves the three to their thoughts.

Snake goes to his desk, opens the top drawer and pulls out a big Cuban cigar. He lights it up and takes a slow drag. "One of the perks" he thinks, "One of the perks."

He then dials the number for the mortuary. Mariah, Bill and Moonbeam can only hear bits and pieces of the conversation through the door. Bill and Mariah's ears are pressed against the door. Words like smuggling, law, remain clear as a bell, but they understand little else. Bill paces back and forth. Mariah looks annoyed.

"Don't go giving me that look Miss Mariah, Snake knows his stuff. He has caught more 'varmints' in these parts single handed than any one else I know."

Mariah answers, "These varmints are not of the common variety. They are foreign, violent, murdering drug smugglers. Not the kid who vandalized a sign with spray paint. I sure hope he knows what he's doing especially since we're now all in the middle of it."

Moonbeam who has remained pretty quiet throughout this visit chimes in, "I will send a message to the spirits to surround us with good fortune. Good fortune for Snake and for us."

Bill says smugly." Moonie, I know you mean well. Just don't get our signals crossed with the killers. Wouldn't want our good fortune to find the wrong people."

Snake seems like he's taking forever to finish his conversation. Mariah begins to pace in the small open space of the warehouse.

Just as she starts, the office door opens. All eyes are now on Snake. He stands still holding onto the cigar with a smug look on his face.

"Well, I talked to old Grimley. Nice guy considering his line of work. He didn't want to help us at first but I read him the riot act about interfering with a federal investigation and suddenly he saw the light. He's ready to join our team! Now you all go back home and follow these instructions exactly. I wrote one letter for each of you. If we can carry this off, we'll have everything under control."

Snake hands Bill the sealed letters. "No-one is to know what is in these instructions except for the three of you and not until the right time and I'll let you know when that is." Bill takes the letters and shakes Snake's hand.

"Thanks, Snake."

Snake smiles, "Relax partner, go back to the beach. Trust me I'll be in touch real soon."

Mariah and Moonbeam take turns giving Snake a big hug. The three leave the small station and go to their car. They are exhausted from the ride, from lack of sleep and from all of the emotional distress their friend's death has caused. They realize that they have to keep going to catch Jocko's killer. They head toward the highway all silent and deep in thought.

CHAPTER THIRTY-EIGHT

As the three make their way back to Seabliss, Snake is busy getting the crates with the urns ready to be picked up for delivery to the mortuary. Once the crates have their original shipping labels back on and look like they are in their original condition, he calls the trucking agent to finalize delivery. The next morning, a large white unmarked truck arrives at the station. The driver provides the necessary paperwork for pickup. Snake releases the containers to the driver knowing that his plan of action has now been put in effect.

As the truck drives off, Snake looks at Joe, "Old boy, I know you think I'm crazy but this may be my only way to stop them. Don't worry; I'm playing along to see where my trail of breadcrumbs will end."

Snake waits about twenty minutes before getting in his jeep to follow the truck to Seabliss. He had to call another station yesterday to arrange for back up in his absence. Dan, his temporary replacement, has already arrived at the Key Isle station and is hiding in the back room. Snake trusts Dan not just with the workload but also with Joe who has stayed with him before. He quickly briefs Dan on the other cases pending, pats Joe on the head, and then leaves. Joe watches out the window as Snake's unmarked jeep pulls away.

Snake has a heavy foot and even though leaving later, manages to arrive in Seabliss right behind the delivery truck. He knows that if he wants to remain anonymous he has to head straight to the mortuary. His first order of business will be to contact Bill by phone shortly after his arrival and advise him to set up a meeting with Moonbeam and Mariah so that they can go over his written instructions carefully and completely. One mistake could blow this whole operation wide open.

Waiting on the other end of the trail for the truck is a very nervous Anna. She wants to pick up the urns as quickly as possible. She frantically paces back and forth in her room hoping that her delivery will come soon and that she can leave for home with the urns.

The normally two to three hour drive to Seabliss has taken almost five hours for the truck carrying the urns. The ride becomes much longer with breakable cargo and the drivers know that they will pay with their lives if the urns are damaged in any way.

The next morning, Anna finally hears the phone ring with good news. "Hey, Miss Anna, it's Dave, Your packages are here. I have all the paperwork ready so you won't have to wait!" Dave is proud of himself for being so customer friendly. Anna thanks him. Relieved, she picks up the phone to notify her accomplice, "They're here, Pacco. Meet me at the store with the rental van."

She immediately heads over to the store where she has Dave give her the paperwork. She signs for the two large crates. Pacco arrives with a dolly just in time to help Dave carefully load the containers into the rental van. "Wow these suckers are heavy. What did they ship? Concrete?" Dave is totally winded not used to physical labor. Pacco is experienced at handling such merchandise from the factory so he just ignores Dave's remarks and says nothing. Once everything is loaded, Pacco plans to meet up with Anna back at the motel but for now, he wants Dave to think of him as a rented driver.

Anna leaves the store by herself and walks back to the motel so as not to cast any suspicion that they are working together.

Once back at the motel, Anna goes to the front desk. She rings the bell on the counter for the clerk. "Excuse me, excuse me, I need assistance." A young male clerk pops his head out of the office. He sees that it's a guest so he walks over to the front desk. "Yes, Mam, how may I help you?"

Anna takes a deep breath, "I have an important delivery coming. I need the packages delivered to my cabin. Will that be a problem if the driver checks in here first?"

"No, M'am, just have them sign in. I will be happy to call your room when they arrive." Anna smiles, "Thank you, I appreciate your help."

Anna has already instructed Pacco to wait a good twenty minutes before arriving and to stop at the office. Anna goes back to her room and waits. She cannot help but pace. Finally, the phone rings. It's the front desk clerk. "M'am, your delivery is here. I will send the truck back. The driver says that they're pretty awkward so I will call a bellman to assist him."

The two men then move the crates into her room. She gladly gives the motel worker a generous tip, thanks Pacco and advises that he leave before the two become connected in any way. He knows that she will call him back when the urns are ready to fill. He goes to the truck and brings in a small black leather satchel. He looks at her as if to give her a silent high five to indicate that their main ingredient has just arrived. Pacco then tells her, "I'll go park the truck on a side street not too far from my motel and then go back to my room. Call me when you are ready."

Just as Pacco arrives back at his room, Anna is calling Alejandro. She pulls the blinds as she makes her call. All she has to say is, "They have arrived."

There is a brief silence and then he replies, "Good, we are well on our way now, my dearest. You know how fragile the urns are. Be careful. Do not try and lift them by yourself. Once you and Pacco have loaded them, call Grimley for his crew to come and pick them up. Did Pacco give you the pouches?"

"He did, I have the two bags in my room now. I will do as we planned and will see you later"

Anna hangs up the phone and then calls Pacco. She lets the phone in his room ring twice, hangs up and calls back as a signal to return. The urns are too heavy for her to complete this task by herself. It takes about fifteen minutes, but she soon hears a knock on the door.

"Who is it?' Anna asks cautiously. "It's me, Pacco, quick, let me in "Anna opens the door and points to the two containers. Pacco takes out his pocketknife and opens the containers with the utmost of care. Anna helps him remove the stuffing and the two lift each urn separately and lay them down on their side on the bed. They now need to open the bottom of each one. Pacco nods his head if to indicate that he is ready for the goods. Anna's hands fumble a bit as she opens the black leather bags and takes out the smaller black velvet bags.

Pacco feels the urn's bottom until he finds the special door. He slides it open. Anna is very nervous and keeps looking around again to make sure that the drapes are drawn and that there are no other eyes on Pacco besides hers. The velvet bags go on top. She reaches for the first bag and starts to put it in the urn. Being a woman, she has to stop and open the black pouch. Beautiful clear sparking large cut emeralds fill her hand. She moves them around in her closed hand. "They are so beautiful."

"Anna stop that nonsense, we have to get to work." Pacco is loading one of the urns. Anna starts to do the other. Still, she holds up one of the pouches and closes her eyes. "Poor Jocko, he worked his whole life and never made what this will bring us in cash. But I know that everyone must take care of himself. I am doing just that"

She pats down the pouches one at a time placing them in the lower part of the urn's cavity. She then reaches into her bra for two velvet bags. Pacco smiles as she places their contents into her right hand before placing them on the nightstand.

Anna is totally mesmerized by the emeralds. They have been something she could never afford. Her beautiful green gems sparkle ever so brightly with what little light breaks through the windows. Each pouch contains two hundred carats of South American emeralds. Some are as large as ten carats, some as small as one. She is the only person who knew that Jocko kept the gems in his cane. He always referred to them as "his retirement fund." She was surprised by how many there are. "Well," Anna thinks, "Before we can spend the money, we have to get them home safely."

Anna carefully returns the emeralds to their pouches and finishes filling each compartment of the urns. She then seals the door with a small plaster kit of the same color. The paste takes about two hours to dry. Pacco turns on the TV to pass the time until the urns will be ready to be placed back in their containers. Once the paste is dry, Anna takes two large round labels from her purse with her factory name on them to cover the bottom of the urns and all of their handiwork.

Pacco then helps her carefully put the urns back in their containers in their upright position and repacks the stuffing. "Anna, we have finished at last. We are almost home. I will leave you now. You know what to do next. Goodbye and good luck." With that, Pacco opens the cottage door, looks both ways hoping not to be seen as he leaves to find his van parked two blocks away. Anna composes herself. Her next move has to be done with the utmost care. She has to call Grimley as the grieving widow and ask to have the urns picked up.

CHAPTER THIRTY-NINE

Anna takes a few minutes to compose herself. After all, stealing from a loved one and smuggling can prove to be emotionally draining. She picks up the phone and dials the mortuary. Her heart is beating so hard she feels as if it could fly out of her chest. She takes a deep breath as she hears Mr. Grimley answer. "Shell Mortuary sending loved ones from one paradise to another for over one hundred years."

"Senor Grimley, this is Anna. The urns have arrived from Mexico. Please send someone to my motel room to pick them up. Your Staff must be extremely careful, as they are very delicate. The urns are all ready to take my Captain home. How soon until final arrangements can be made?"

Grimley pauses for a few seconds and then asks "Would you mind holding for a few minutes while I look that up, my dear?" Anna responds "No" even though every minute seems like an eternity to her.

Grimley's hold serves an important purpose. It seems that he has to consult with his new associate. This associate has a vested interest in the outcome of the arrangements; his name is Stanley Ringster.

Grimley remains silent as he points to the phone as if to signal Snake that it's Anna on the line. Snake gives him a nod as a signal to continue.

"Anna, my dear sweet lady, I am so sorry about the hold. How are you? Your brave Captain is now ready to go home. Since his remains are leaving the country, I will have some paperwork for you to complete and sign for customs. If I may and I want to be delicate, there is also the matter of our bill. It must be paid in full by cashier's check or cash before I can let the urns leave the mortuary. I do hope you understand that it is hard to find people once they have left the US for Mexico. Oh, and did I mention that both parties, you and Alejandro, must be present to sign the documents since the urns are being shipped in separate containers."

Grimley senses that he is on a roll so he continues. "The Captain's son, I take it, has arrived. Hasn't he? We cannot proceed without him"

Anna is quick to respond, "He has, Mr. Grimley, and he will be the one making payment."

Grimley repeats part of her answer for Snake's benefit, "That's wonderful Jocko's son is here. As I said before, I would not be able to proceed with our services as well as the shipping requirements unless the both of you are present. I will send my assistant over to pick up the urns shortly. Please watch for my vehicle. It has the mortuary name on it in gold letters."

"I will" Anna replies." I do understand about the paperwork and will tell Alejandro that Jocko has been cremated and we may proceed with his final arrangements. His son will make a cash payment when we come for a private service before removing the urns."

Mr. Grimley responds, "That will be fine, Ms. Anna. Thank you for understanding. One of my assistants has already left and will be right over to help you."

Anna feels a bit relieved that someone on this island is efficient; this seemingly long ordeal will finally be over. She tells Grimley, "Thank you," hangs up the phone and plops down on the large wicker chair near the window to steal a moment's rest.

Now that the urns have been repacked, Anna feels comfortable opening the drapes to let the warm sunlight in. She sits up in the large white wicker fan chair soaking in its healing heat as she waits for Grimley's assistant. It doesn't take very long for Anna to see a large black hearse pull up to her motel door. The driver's door opens, a tall lanky mortuary attendant steps out wearing leather boots and dressed in a dark suit. The tall gentleman pulls out a stainless steel dolly. She quickly hears a knock at her door. " Ma'am, Mr. Grimley sent me to assist you," the mortuary attendant says with a deep southern drawl.

"Please come in," Anna answers as she opens the door and points to the two containers. The attendant carefully takes one out at a time on the gurney loading each of them into the back part of the hearse.

"Please sign here, M'am. Mr. Grimley will call you when everything is ready. He said to tell you that he should be ready to conduct your private service tomorrow, Wednesday afternoon, at three thirty. He said, however, to wait for his call in the morning to confirm the precise time. Please take care. It's been my pleasure to serve you."

With that, the tall lanky attendant gets in the hearse, checks his rear view mirror to make sure that he is not being followed and heads back to the mortuary. Anna watches from the window. After the truck leaves her sight, she collapses on the bed emotionally exhausted.

From the very second that Mariah, Bill and Moonbeam hit the sands of Seabliss, they all went back to work at their normal jobs. Snake finally called a couple of days ago leaving a cryptic message on Bill's answering machine. "It's Snake. Read the book."

After Bill hears the message, he contacts Moonbeam and Mariah. The three hold a secret meeting at a scenic overlook of a county park just over the main bridge to the island, Bill brings the three letters and passes each out to its rightful owner. They quietly read and hopefully memorize Snake's instructions.

"Do you really think we can pull this off?' Mariah asks.

Bill answers confidently, "Honey with Snake in our corner, we can do practically anything."

"I saw a serpent in my dream last night," Moonbeam chimes in, "He was coiled and ready to attack. His venom was filled with good. We must do this for Jocko."

Mariah takes a deep breath. "OK I'm ready."

"We're all ready, now go back to work and wait for my call," Bill tells them.

The three part ways hopeful that their next get-together will be to capture Jocko's killers.

No one is more anxious than Bill. He has been checking in with Grimley by phone on a regular basis. He knows that Snake is there but does not want to be connected with him. Today, Mr. Grimley finally calls. "Bill, this is Mr. Grimley. The project is due tomorrow at three thirty. I'm sure that you and your assistants will want to arrive early."

Then, Bill quickly calls Mariah who calls Moonbeam. By communicating in this order, nothing seems unusual. The three are instructed through Bill to meet at the mortuary at 2:00 Wednesday afternoon and to remember their lines.

For Mariah, tomorrow seems like an eternity. She cannot concentrate at the store. She is extremely restless and has trouble sleeping. Her mind is focused on Jocko's killer. She tosses and turns wondering if the plans will work. Wednesday morning finally arrives. Mariah takes a quick wake up shower and she and Spike go to work at her store as usual. Of course, she is nervous. She goes to her office to call Moonbeam. It's too early for Moonbeam to get a business call so she answers the phone herself.

"Hey, Moonie, Mariah. I couldn't sleep. I can't concentrate. I just hope I don't mess up anything. I came in the back office because people notice that I'm not myself. Even Danny the plumber, who needed to know who played the lead in 'Mame' found it hard to believe that I couldn't remember. I really couldn't! Imagine that! Even the most mundane actions like making change or listening to local gossip make my head swim!"

Moonbeam, also trying to keep her day seem as normal as possible, can relate. "Mariah, I know just how you feel. I opened my door much earlier than usual today. I probably shouldn't have because Daisy Fletcher spotted me doing that from across the street and came right over to see if I could contact her dead mother for advice. Her college age son wants to study abroad next semester and she doesn't want him to go that far from home."

"I tried and tried but I couldn't reach the great beyond. She got very antsy as I called the spirits several times trying desperately to reach her mother. I finally had to apologize and not charge her. I told her to come back tomorrow when there should not be as much cosmic interference and I will reach her mother for free. Mrs. Fletcher was not happy. She needed her mother's advice. She saw how hard I tried. She wanted to understand, but I know I messed up. I just can't get Jocko off my mind! Oops UPS is here with my crystals, Gotta go. See you at two."

Bill is the most relaxed of the three. He leans back in his chair. "I know if old Snake is involved, everything is under control. We all just need to follow his directions. No one in Seabliss has ever seen him or heard of him before. He's slick. Grimley even said he was impressed when he saw how easily Snake entered the mortuary through the back door carrying a dark suit just like a newly hired attendant."

Bill is pleased that Grimley now has the proper attitude to help because everything seems to be going right on schedule. At quarter to two, Bill calls Mariah and tells her to meet him at "G's." He sounds very serious as he adds, "Call Moonie and don't forget the props."

Mariah has to call from the store phone and relay a cryptic message to Moonbeam that neither Shane nor her customers will figure out. "M this is ditto. The show is ready to start. Don't be late and don't forget the popcorn."

Mariah then picks up her tote bag with "Ghostbusters" embossed on the front and starts to pack some things that she knows that she will need. Spike starts to wag his tail as if he is going with her but she tells him, "Be a good boy and watch the store. I'll be back soon, sweetie."

Mariah then looks at Shane, "Shane, I have to go run some errands. I'm leaving Spike with you. Take good care of him." Shane thinks her composure a bit serious but attributes it to a possible headache. "OK boss" Shane responds knowing that her errands could take a few hours.

Mariah then leaves the store, slides into in her Mustang and heads to the Shell Mortuary.

Moonbeam is preparing to leave for Grimley's as well. She turns her open sign around and also puts a few things in her black velvet tote bag with a gold crescent moon and stars embroidered on it. She locks up and starts to walk to Grimley's. She has a silk rose colored scarf over her head and looks down at the sidewalk so as to discourage people from talking to her. She does not want them to diminish her powers or lose her concentration.

All three of Jocko's friends arrive individually and as planned. Moonbeam actually arrives two minutes ahead of Mariah. She knocks on the front door nervously awaiting Mr. Grimley.

Bill is already in the building but in the preparation room with Snake. He has some magic to perform himself before he can change into a black suit. Mariah is the last to arrive as planned. She parks her car out of sight around the corner and also walks in the front door, her head covered by a rose colored scarf as well.

CHAPTER FORTY
ASHES TO ASHES

After Mr. Grimley greets Moonbeam in his traditional manner, he then escorts her into the large open room that is reserved for special services. He always leaves seven rows of chairs set up for any emergency or impromptu memorials. He points to the front of the room where the urns will be placed. Moonbeam follows his lead and takes a seat not too far back from the urns' future site.

A few short minutes later, there is another knock. Mariah arrives. Grimley escorts her into the same room where she takes her place further back and on the other side of the room from Moonbeam so as not to appear connected. Grimley wishes both women well as he slides the stained glass doors shut, "If you ladies need anything, I will be in and out." He then leaves them alone.

Grimley's next task is in the preparation room to check on Bill and Snake's progress. They have been busy burning some large cardboard boxes and old newspapers for ashes. Grimley looks into the furnace and gives a nod of approval to Snake.

"Hey Bill, think we might have enough now Let's start." Snake looks at the ashes and carefully pushes them into two sections with his shovel. He begins to scoop up the ashes and to fill the first urn. They fill both the urns with equal amounts of paper ashes and not Jocko's. They carefully place the lids on the urns but do not seal them.

Bill looks at his watch. "Hey man, we better get a move on. It's getting close." The two men quickly change into their dark suits. Looking very proper and serious, they solemnly carry the urns filled with paper ashes into the service room. Bill and Snake carefully lift them onto two large black round pods. The pods are designed to rotate and operate similar to a large automatic lazy susan. Grimley had them built as a special touch to rotate extra large floral arrangements. They would not ordinarily be used for a cremation service but this service is far from ordinary.

The pods are located on both sides of a large hand carved antique sideboard. Since the urns are not sealed on the top, Snake is able to open each one and place some of the ashes in his hand. He smears the ashes on the table and down the side of each urn.

Moonbeam carefully watches Snake. She realizes that the time for the service is quickly approaching. She reaches into her velvet bag and pulls out two green silk scarves. She specifically selected the color green hoping to subconsciously connect the emeralds to Jocko's ashes in the killer's mind. Moonbeam slowly walks over to the sideboard and places one on each urn arranging them so they act as a partial drape covering a good portion of each pod.

Bill and Snake turn in unison and walk slowly back to the preparation room to clean themselves up from the ashes. In case someone is watching, the service must appear to take place as it usually would. Snake is almost unrecognizable in a suit, clean-shaven, and wearing cologne. Bill puts his uniform back on. He hopes that by the time Anna and her friends see him in his normal garb, they'll know that they're in deep trouble.

Meanwhile back in the service room, Moonbeam is still at work. She must cover up her identity as much as possible. After all, she has by now met all of them. She pulls a black jacket out of her bag and puts it on. She gives another one to Mariah who does the same. The two women go to their planned places. They sit in chairs in different sections of the room on opposite aisles. They are still wearing scarves on their heads and look down. They sit with their backs to the entrance and slump their shoulders so as not to call attention to themselves.

Mariah gives Moonbeam a thumbs up "Ready Moonie it's almost 3:30. Let's do this for Jocko." Moonbeam winks smiling back, "Ready."

Just then they hear the saddened tones of Grimley's front door bell. Snake is the first on the scene and answers the door. Mariah and Moonbeam are able to hear him greet the first mourner.

"Please come in, M'am" Snake says respectively. Anna enters dressed in a very fitted black dress looking as beautiful as ever.

Snake's voice is calming. "We are deeply sorry for your loss. Won't you please follow me to Mr. Grimley's office? I believe that he has paperwork for you to complete."

Anna answers quietly, "Of course. Thank you. Weren't you the one who came to pick up the urns?

"Yes M'am." Snake responds as the door tones sound again.

"Wait right here for me M'am. I'll get that as well. It might be the captain's son. We can all go together." Snake opens the heavy door and a tall thin handsome Hispanic gentleman is there.

Snake immediately recognizes Alejandro from international wanted posters. Snake is salivating at the thought of bringing him down. "You, my friend," he thinks, "Are the king of drug lords; the catch of all catches…Ha…just think it'll be my venom that finally does you in."

Snake snaps out of his daydream speaking slowly, "Welcome sir. You must be Jocko's son? Ms. Anna has already arrived. If you would be so kind, please accompany me to Mr. Grimley's office. Ms. Anna is waiting for us in the hallway."

Snake should have been nicknamed "Chameleon"; he's a good imposter, a very good one. Even old Mr. Grimley is impressed, so much so that Grimley told Snake that if he ever retires from law enforcement, he would hire him on the spot.

"Yes, yes I am Jocko's son," Alejandro answers. "Anna is already here then?' he asks. "Yes sir, as I said, she is waiting for you. Please follow me." Snake takes Alejandro down the same hall to meet up with Anna. The three then proceed to Grimley's office.

CHAPTER FORTY-ONE

Grimley straightens his tie as he nervously awaits his two visitors. The mortuary is very quiet giving Grimley time to think.

"I come from a long line of morticians. This involves the honor of my family name. I am an honest man and shudder at the thought of being involved with drug money. Snake assured me that I am doing my civic duty. I guess I trust him; otherwise I would nix the whole thing."

Besides the money, Grimley is concerned about safety. He would be horrified if anyone were to get hurt in his peaceful establishment. He knows that federal agents are there as back up and hopes that everything goes as planned.

Grimley looks down at his desk. All of the necessary paperwork is ready. Grimley may not like his part but he knows what he has to do. He can hear footsteps on the hardwood floors approaching. Snake knocks slowly on the office door. Grimley sits up straight in his desk chair and says, "Please come in." He stands courteously when Anna and Alejandro enter.

Grimley walks over to greet Anna first and places her hands in his. "Please come over and sit down. I know how painful this must be for you. We can take care of this quickly. I need both signatures on the lines highlighted."

Grimley hands them each a pen and watches as each of them sign. He asks his next question as delicately as possible. "I have to ask Madam, did Alejandro bring the payment?"

Snake stays in Grimley's office and watches from the back of the room as all of this transpires. Usually, Grimley would rather his meetings remain private between himself and his clients, but this one is an exception. He knows how dangerous Alejandro is and is comforted by the fact that Snake carries a concealed weapon.

Anna pauses for a minute and then answers Grimley's question. "Yes, he has."

"Mr. Grimley, as Jocko's son, I have brought the money and am honored to pay for his service." Alejandro reaches into his pocket. Snake is on guard. He pulls out $2000 in cash and places it on Grimley's big desk. Grimley counts the funds just as he would normally do and then turns to put the money into his safe. He then writes out a receipt for Alejandro, "Thank you. We are all set now, Mr. Alejandro." Grimley has a way of saying his long Spanish name slowly rolling the R.

Getting up from his chair, Mr. Grimley expresses his sympathy again and adds, "It's now time to take your loved one home. Please follow me and we will begin the community service for Captain Jocko."

Anna looks a bit surprised. "We did not request a public service. We specifically asked for a private one."

Grimley answers quickly, "I know but I am doing it gratis as a favor to a beloved member of our island community. I hope that you don't mind."

"Of course not," Anna responds quickly not wanting to cause concern. "I know how much Jocko was loved here."

"Good, then let us go to his service." The mortician escorts the couple out of his office. He opens the door to the room where the service is scheduled and lets both of them in.

Grimley asks, "Are you expecting anyone else to meet you here to view the urns?"

Anna is quick to respond, "Yes, Jocko's trusted foreman, Pacco. He should be here any minute."

As soon as Anna finishes her sentence, the doorbell rings one more time. Snake eagerly answers the door and escorts the rotund and somewhat surprised Pacco into the service room. Once Pacco is in the room, Snake positions himself in the back to assist Grimley as needed.

CHAPTER FORTY-TWO
THE IMPORTANCE OF BEING URNS

Anna's first glance upon entering the room is of the stately urns. Her eyes are wide with tears. "Oh my, how beautiful they are. Jocko would have loved them. The green drapes are lovely as well. Jocko always said that green was his favorite color."

She pauses a moment trying to gain her composure. She starts to cry maybe out of love, maybe from guilt, in front of Pacco and Alejandro. They both console her. Snake offers her a handkerchief as he places one of her arms in his and escorts her to one of the front row seats. Anna stops suddenly when she passes the two women seated in the back. Because of their scarves, Anna is unable to see their faces. Snake notices how quickly Anna is able to regain her composure.

"Who are these people? I thought that I made it explicitly clear that when we came, no one else should be here." She turns and snaps at Snake who remains perfectly composed.

"They are members of our island community who have been chosen to represent the entire community at the service." Snake answers quickly and hopes that makes sense to Anna.

"Yes, yes, just as Senor Grimley said," Anna remembers nervously.

Snake senses that Alejandro is getting a bit anxious with Anna's outburst. He quietly turns midway down the aisle and motions to Alejandro to stay there and wait for him to come back and get him. He then takes Anna by the arm again and escorts her to the front row of chairs. He seats her nearest the urns.

He gently whispers in Anna's ear, "Oh Madam, do not worry. They are just local woman who wish to pay their respects. The Captain had many female admirers. I am sure that they will leave quietly when the proper time comes. With that Snake pats Anna's hand and then heads to the back of the room and proceeds to escort Pacco to his chair next to Anna.

He talks to Pacco in a low voice, "Mr. Grimley wants to give you all a few minutes to pay your respects in private. I will seat Alejandro now and will leave you to pay your respects." He makes sure that Anna is still all right and then returns to Alejandro to take him to the seat next to Pacco.

Alejandro walks with Snake, sits down next to Pacco. Snake takes another handkerchief from his pocket to give to Anna. Alejandro then helps her up and takes her to view the urns. Unsure of what they should do, they both kneel down in respect in front of the urns.

Mariah, watching the pair quietly, reaches into her tote and pulls out a camcorder. She keeps it hidden temporarily placing it on her lap.

From the back of the room, Grimley is watching nervously. He keeps his composure as he starts to walk down the small main aisle to the front. He looks as sullen as usual and carries his service book holding it close to his chest perhaps worried about stray bullets.

Once up front, he immediately goes over to Anna and Alejandro helping them to their feet. He talks quietly with them for a few minutes and then helps them back to their seats. Grimley extends a hand and then greets Pacco as Snake makes his way to the front of the room to take his place in back of the urns. Snake folds his hands behind him. He may appear to be staring at the far wall but he is really taking in the entire situation much like a secret service agent does when guarding the President. Grimley motions for the guests to be seated,

"Everyone, please be seated so that we may begin. Anna and Alejandro you know how deeply sorry I am for your loss. We are here to remember the life of a wonderful and loving man. In doing so, I have asked one of his dearest friends to tape the service for you so that you might take the service back to the factory and show your workers what a nice farewell Seabliss provided for Captain Jocko. This young lady has volunteered as a friend and does not want to be paid. Is that all right with you both?"

Anna looks surprised. Alejandro does not ruffle as easily and replies "Very well. I'm sure that the workers will appreciate this."

Mariah, proudly making her film debut, stands up and walks slowly toward the urns filming as she goes. Mr. Grimley has already begun reading from his service book. As soon as Mariah nears the front, Moonbeam stands up, raises her arms in the air, and starts to wail. She is uncontrollable. Her cries are so loud that she drowns out Mr. Grimley's voice. "Oh my Jocko. The spirits told me that you came too early. Who is responsible for this? I ask again. Who? Show them to me."

Anna recognizes Moonbeam. "She's the psychic! Why is she here?"

Alejandro becomes angry at Moonbeam's dramatic display, "Get her out of here. She is disrespectful to my father," he yells," She will ruin the service!"

Grimley looks up from his book. With his reading glasses at the bottom of his nose, he motions to Moonbeam to be quiet and sit down. Moonbeam quiets down. After being seated again, she pulls an object from her black velvet bag. It is a large crystal ball, one that can fractionalize light, spreading colors like thin lasers throughout the room. She holds the crystal ball up to the light in the room. Its rays are almost blinding.

Moonbeam starts to speak again. Her speech pattern is slow as if possessed. "I had a vision. I had a very dark vision. A deep dark vision about a man I know. He was an old man, a kind man, and a man of the sea. Oh, Alas, green glass, I see that he is now no more!"

Snake is still standing in the front of the room. Anna goes to him and instructs him firmly, "Please remove her. She is disrupting the service." Snake nods his head and goes over to grab Moonbeam's arm. Without being noticed, he touches his side pocket as he leaves the podium. Just then the urns start to rotate violently on the pods.

Moonbeam by now appears to be deranged. She yells as Snake grabs her arm. "Stop. Stop you demon. Don't touch me" Moonbeam manages to pull her arm free rather easily. She points dramatically to the front, "Look at the urns, they know that I tell the truth. The man I saw walked with a cane filled with beautiful green glass and loved the people who betrayed him. The man spoke to me in my vision and said 'Help me! Help me!!' That is why I am here. To help the old man."

By now, Moonbeam knows that she is on a role. She is unstoppable. She begins acting like a crazed person running to the front and placing her crystal ball between the urns. She lifts her arms in the air and runs around the urns as if performing an ancient ritual. "Help me I heard him say. Someone has killed me! Find them. Find them. I know that they are all here in this room."

The urns are still rotating on the table. Snake touches his pocket again and increases their speed making some of the ashes spill from the top. The urns start to wobble. If they should fall off of the pods and break, Anna and Alejandro fear that the secret compartments will release all of the emeralds.

Alejandro by now is angry, very angry. "Get these disrespectful charlatans out of here now or I will if I have to kill them both." The look in his eyes says it all.

Snake grabs onto Moonbeam again. He touches his pocket to slow the urns down to a stop. Moonbeam is still wailing and evades his touch. She becomes quiet as a chill runs down her spine.

This time, she's not afraid. She feels her head being yanked back sharply. Moonbeam hates that feeling but she knows it's Jocko's spirit.

"Jocko, it's you isn't it. Tell me what to do."

Everyone except for Bill and Snake gasps at the thought of a visitor from the great beyond.

Moonbeam's head is jerked from side to side. She looks like she is in a trance, her eyes fixed on Anna. She opens her mouth. In a familiar voice that is not hers, she speaks slowly, "I told you before. I know that I did not need two needles. The woman I love told me that it would be all right. That she missed the first time. Oh I'm so miserable. I loved her and trusted her. She put poison in the other needle and I let her inject me with her venom unaware. They killed me! They killed me! All for my emeralds!"

Moonbeam by now is shouting. Angry, the voice continues, "How could they? How could they? I trusted two of them."

Mr. Grimley does not know what to make of the whole thing. He has stepped down and moved to the side of the room.

Alejandro stands up. He is surprised by Moonbeam's channeling. Sounding brave he looks at Snake. "This is not a service. This is nonsense. I say get rid of them now. "He means business as he pulls a gun from his jacket pocket and grabs Moonbeam around the neck. He points the gun barrel at her head.

The voice begins to speak again. "Your gun does not scare me. I know who you really are. Tell them what you did. Tell them who you are." Alejandro is surprised by Moonbeam's tenacity but not impressed.

Anna gets up and tries to calm him down. "Alejandro, let her go she is just some crazy local woman. Let's get Jocko's remains and get out of here." Anna goes on" Look at my Jocko's ashes; they are spilling all over the floor. Remember that we have a boat to meet. Mr. Grimley, I am deeply saddened by today. We must leave right now." Anna gives Alejandro a look as if to say that they are almost home. Don't mess it up now.

Alejandro would have been all too happy to shoot Moonbeam, but remembering the precious cargo and the money involved, puts the gun away. Snake keeps a close eye on him from the other side of the room. Bill, in uniform, is waiting behind the door.

As soon as Alejandro lets Moonbeam go, she shakes herself back to normal. Remembering the actual plan, she goes to the window and opens the drapes a crack to let a little of the light in. The light hits the crystal ball again at just the right spot almost blinding the attendees with its colorful rays. She then lifts her arms again and grabs one as if having a severe cramp. "Oh my, look, he is sending a message from beyond. Look at what he sent us!" Moonbeam is amazing considering that she has just channeled a spirit and had a gun pointed to her head. She is more angry at them for killing Jocko then scared and is determined to put these three away for good.

She tells herself, "I have to finish Snake's plan and give the best performance of my life for Jocko." She then opens her right hand and tiny fragments of green crystals fall out. They too glimmer in the light. By now Alejandro has seen enough. "This is blasphemy. The poor man is dead. This is his service. What kind of people do things like this?"

Snake then touches his pocket again to start the urns rotating at fast speed. This time, those urns really rip. Anna not thinking blurts out, "Stop this, Stop this, they will break and we will lose the emeralds! We would have killed Jocko for nothing. Luis, you must do something to stop them!"

Anna covers her mouth realizing what she just said. Everyone now knows who they are. Luis reaches in his pocket and quickly pulls out his gun. "I've had enough of your charades. Grimley, get those urns ready for travel." Grimley does not move. He is scared out of his mind by the sight of the gun.

Snake slows the urns down to a stop as Luis points his gun around the room. He instructs Anna and Pacco to go get the urns. Luis asks, "Who gave you the right to go through Jocko's things? You think that you're smart. If you were that smart you would never have let me in. Those emeralds are ours. You may think that you can outsmart us for the rewards and scare us off but you can't. I will kill all of you one at a time starting with that crazy one." Luis points to Moonbeam

Anna grabs Mariah's camera and throws it to the ground. Mariah left it on so it is still recording. Pacco goes to the front and carefully takes each of the urns off of their respective pods. Snake keeps his post in the front of the room knowing that Bill has the back.

Mariah is mad, "You are the charlatans. First you kill Jocko then take his emeralds, now you want to commit murder in the mortuary but it won't work. We are not afraid of you. Any of you three!"

Luis laughs a wicked laugh, "You may not be afraid but you do know too much. Since everyone in this room is about to die I will tell you this much. Yes, we did kill Jocko but not just for the emeralds; we want to own the plant together. I got the poison. Anna switched the needles and injected him. Pacco cleaned out his cane. He did love Anna you know, foolish old man that he was."

Anna throws her head back and laughs an equally wicked laugh. "How could you believe that I was still in love with that old bird? I wanted his money. This is not all of his booty. There are emeralds on their way back to Mexico now in TV monitors." She reaches in her purse and pulls out a pistol, one that she aims at Mariah. "You, you are the reason for this mess. I knew that you were trouble the first time I met you in Jocko's apartment. I want to kill you first." She cocks the trigger and waves to Pacco to pick up an urn. Pacco does just that. He begins to drag it to the back of the room to take outside.

Snake on guard runs to the back of the room and blocks the door. He quickly reaches for his ankle. He grabs his concealed weapon. Bill kicks the door open. Accompanied by two special FBI agents, his gun is drawn. "Not so fast. Drop the guns. Drop the urn. Or it will be your turn to die."

Bill focuses his aim on Luis; Snake watches Anna. The FBI watches both. Outgunned and scared out his mind, Pacco puts the urn down and places his hands in the air.

"Mariah did you leave the camcorder on before you dropped it?" Snake asks with a smile. Mariah shakes her head yes. "Well my amigos, we have your confession on tape; an unsolicited confession at that for smuggling, robbery and murder." Snake shoots his weapon at the ceiling as a warning. "That shot, my friends, triggers Grimley's alarm. The alarm now signals more federal agents waiting as back up. You three criminal masterminds don't think that ol' Snake would do a job like this without arranging for a plenty of back up."

"Put those weapons down." His warning is well heard as the door to the room opens again, this time with four armed federal agents coming in to get Anna, Luis, and Pacco. Anna drops her gun first. Luis is reticent. After all he is the drug lord. But it's hard to hold out with Bill and two federal agents pointing their weapons directly at him. Snake reads Anna her rights and then handcuffs her. Bill and crew swarm Luis. They tackle him to the ground making him drop his gun. They read him his rights as they handcuff him as well. Pacco is easy not wanting to be hurt.

"You can't hold us you know," Luis yells as the agents lift him to his feet.

Snake smiles, "You can think that all you want. Trust me, Luis, when your federal government finds out who I have in custody, I wouldn't want to go to the prison where they'll be sending you."

"But first, you get to stay in Florida a little longer where you will be tried for murder. We kill murderers here by lethal injection, you know. How's that for justice?"

The four federal agents walk the trio out of Grimley's mortuary. Luis all the while is trying to get free. "I have the best lawyers money can buy in Miami. This will not stick, you slimy bastards."

Snake just smiles, "I have enough on you, your helper, and your little sweetie to put all of you on death row. You all will never see the light of day again. Good riddance." Bill and Snake follow the federal agents out to their cars for added support. When they arrive back in the room, they see Mariah collapsed in a chair and Moonbeam reading tarot cards for Mr. Grimley. It's her way of dealing with stress.

Mariah looks at Snake and Bill "OK. You two can thank us now."

Snake and Bill look at each other and smile,

"I thought that sting would never end. Now let's take a minute to catch our breaths, and then let's honor Jocko the right way." Mariah says wearily. Mr. Grimley agrees.

They all sit for a few minutes before Mr. Grimley escorts them into a smaller side room where a beautiful stainless steel urn inscribed "Our Captain" is on the center table.

Mariah, Bill, Snake, and Moonbeam pay their respects as the door bolts open. They turn to see Brady enter with Spike on a leash. "Snake told me what happened on the radio. I thought Spike would like to share in this as well."

Spike is let off of his leash. He approaches the urn carefully and sniffs it. He then lies down in front of it just as if the Captain was still there with him.

The service is heartfelt and appropriate. Mr. Grimley reads from the traditional service book. When he finishes, Mariah speaks, "For Spike and me, Captain Jocko was the best friend anyone could ever want. We'll miss him, his laugh, his stories and his advice. Rest in peace, my dear Captain."

After the service, Mr. Grimley assures Mariah that Jocko's remains will be sent to his village in Mexico for a proper burial; one that he would have wanted. Mr. Grimley also tells her that his mortuary would be honored to pay for Jocko's final arrangements. After all, Jocko was his friend as well. Mariah's eyes swell with tears as she gives Grimley a big hug of gratitude "I'll miss Jocko but I always will remember what you did for him."

CHAPTER FORTY-THREE
TWO WEEKS LATER

The loyal and honest workers at Jocko's plant are ready to welcome Jocko home. His passing saddens them, but his funeral mass in the beautiful church in the square is comforting to them. It is even more comforting for them to know that Luis is in jail and will not be their boss. The local priest announced that he allocated a crypt in the church for Jocko's burial, one that is usually saved for clergy, because of the good that Jocko brought their small village.

The first shipment of stolen emeralds was stopped before it reached Mexico and the others have been taken out of the urns that were loaded with the cardboard ashes. Mariah discovers a safe deposit key among Jocko's possessions and with Bill's assistance and the court's approval opens it to find his will. Of course, Anna was the chief beneficiary but she since can no longer inherit, Jocko made provisions for whatever reason that if Anna was not able to be the beneficiary then his plant was to be divided equally among three of his most loyal workers. He knew who they were and named them specifically. They were to join together to form one company. In the event Anna could not receive the emeralds, they were to go to a local Mexican Children's hospital to sell and use the proceeds for improvements and new equipment. Of course the sly old sailor keeping in character made provisions for this event to be tightly monitored by U.S. and Mexican attorneys.

To Mariah's surprise, Jocko left her his small condo on the island and his tiny Oceanside cottage in Mexico for all of the care and concern she showed him throughout their years of friendship.

Since all of this happened, Mariah has received many letters of thanks from the villagers and many invitations to visit Ojuana. They all wrote that they would treat her like Jocko's daughter.

Since Mariah always discusses everything with Spike, she takes him for a ride to the quiet end of the island. There watching the beach and Gulf, she reads her last batch of letters and invitations to him out loud. He tilts his head and wags his tail before Mariah turns her car around and leaves her prime parking space. "Ready to go home, boy. Don't know about you, but I sure am. We can decide what to do next after a short rest." Spike and Mariah then proceed to drive home down the gulf front boulevard their hearts filled with love and their minds filled with hope.

###